SONG BOOK

Norrin M. Ripsman

Cassowary Publications

Philadelphia

Copyright © 2023 by Norrin M. Ripsman

United States copyright registration numbers
TXu-2-409-594 & TXu-2-409-602

First paperback edition April 2024

Book design by Dawn Black

Cover design by Jean-Pierre Agrang

ISBN 978-0-9601245-3-4 (paperback)

To my father, **Michael Ripsman,**
who always wanted to write,
but never found the time.

Table of Contents

Foreword

The evocative poetry of classic rock songs, which has always captured my imagination, was the inspiration for this collection. Each story was either inspired by some of the compositions that move me the most or is indelibly linked in my mind with the texture or lyrics of particular songs. Moreover, like myself, the characters themselves often interact with the world through the prism of these lyrics, often quoting them directly or selecting music to mirror their frames of mind. I therefore conceived of this collection as my *Song Book*. I began each story with a classic rock/folk epigraph that captured an essential mood of the story, if not its central theme. I also allowed my characters to express their love of music freely, as I do myself.

Unfortunately, this artistic vision crashed against the rocky shoal of the music industry. When I sought permission to publish the relevant song lyrics – some as short as a single line – I was informed that it would cost several thousand dollars to publish them. That was simply not practicable for a small-market publication like this.

After much agonizing about whether this was, in effect, the death knell for my *Song Book* – I felt much like my character Simon in "Speculation," whose frustration with business considerations getting in the way of the beauty of art is palpable – I decided to remain as true to the original concept as possible. Although I have sadly removed the epigraphs and the direct quotations in the stories, I have maintained the texture and the moods they inspire. Where the lyrics actually played an important role in driving a story forward, I supplemented my own 'classic rock' lyrics, in the form of songs by fictional rock groups the Chocolate Bullfrogs and the Melancholy Grapes. In addition, I include an Appendix listing the sources of the epigraphs for each story. Hopefully, this has left the music of the *Song Book* intact.

I owe debts of gratitude to my mother, my daughters and my good friends Edann Brady, Jermaine Brinkley, Annette Freyberg-Inan, Michael Lipson, Jeff Taliaferro, Monique and Stephen Wallace, and Ron Wener, who read earlier drafts of some of these stories. Their encouragement and feedback helped me turn a rough beginning into a final product. Above all, I am eternally grateful to my wife, Nathalie, for all her love and support. She put aside writing her own plays to read several drafts of this book and my *The Oracle of Spring Garden Road* novel manuscript, in the process helping me correct sour notes and flat prose. Without her, there would be no *Song Book* and no music in my life.

Norrin M. Ripsman

Philadelphia, PA

November 2023

A Weekend at the Cottage

He closed his eyes and inevitably the image returned, as it had most nights over the previous month: the pine coffin, a large white cross across its top, lowered by pullies into the freshly-dug grave. He could remember the rest. The overcast April sky; the damp, muddy ground with the remnants of winter's snow; the bitter wind; sombre mourners gathered around. But it was the lowering of the coffin that he kept seeing, that haunted him, wouldn't let him sleep.

How long will this go on? he brooded. He threw off his duvet comforter and stumbled out of bed into his dog-eared slippers. As usual, he fumbled for the light switch and wandered down the hall of his Sherbrooke Street condominium to the kitchen for a glass of port. After a few sips, he reached for his telephone. A quarter to two. *Should I disturb her? Probably not*, he decided, but punched in her number anyway. After four rings, it went straight to her voicemail. He disconnected without leaving a message, disappointed. A few minutes later she called back.

"I was in bed, Oliver," her jasmine voice said drowsily. "Are you alright?"

"No…. I don't know…. I still can't sleep."

"Is it still the coffin?" she asked.

"Yes. I can't get it out of my head. It's seared onto my retinas," Oliver replied, rubbing an itchy patch behind his ear.

"Look. It's normal. You lost your brother. You're allowed to feel sad."

"But that's just it. I don't really feel sad. I don't really feel *anything*," he protested. "It's like I'm numb,"

"You feel *something*, or else you wouldn't be bothered by his funeral, the sight of his coffin," she said gently.

"Listen. Paul and I were identical twins. We had the kind of connection you read about with twins. He'd catch a cold and I'd sneeze. I knew when he was in love and when he'd had his heart broken again before he even told me…."

"Your relationship was very special," she interjected.

"Yet he got sick in Vancouver – was deathly ill for over a week – and *I didn't have an inkling!* He died without me knowing. I was on the slopes at Mont Tremblant and didn't know the difference. *How can that be?*" he bemoaned.

She was silent at the other end of the line, no doubt discouraged that she was unable to find the magic formula to console him. How *can* you console someone on a loss like that? Eventually she settled on, "You can't beat yourself up about it."

"And why can't I cry?" he continued as if he hadn't heard her. "He's been dead over a month now – my brother, my *twin*, my closest friend – and I still haven't shed a tear. Am I inhuman? A monster?"

"Of course not! You need to give it time. You've suffered a terrible loss. It's your duty to grieve, but you don't know how. There's no roadmap for you to follow. Everyone needs to mourn differently. It's hard work, but you must figure out how to do your duty in your own way." She paused and he could picture the nostalgic smile on her lips as she continued, "My father used to repeat a Japanese proverb: duty is heavy as a mountain, but death is lighter than a feather."

"I would have liked to have met him," he said softly.

"But maybe you can't find your path to grieving alone in your apartment. I have an idea. We're going up to the cottage near Saint-Sauveur over the weekend. Why don't you join us?" she offered.

He hesitated. *It wouldn't be proper*, he thought. *I'd be intruding.* Yet the idea appealed to him. "I'd love to," he said at last.

"Wonderful!" she said. "Now let's both try to get some sleep."

"Hanako…." His voice trailed off.

"Yes?"

"Thank you."

Oliver left work early that Friday. As a notary in his own small private firm, he was able to make his own hours. Although he had initially scheduled a real estate transaction for that afternoon, he asked his secretary to postpone it until the following Monday to permit his departure.

With the first warm weekend of the season forecasted, traffic on Autoroute 15 was painfully slow. Nonetheless, it eased up after Saint-Jérome, and by 5:00PM he pulled up at the cottage, nestled between a small forest and a pristine lake. Inhaling the sweet country air deeply, he retrieved his overnight bag and an excellent bottle of Australian Shiraz from the trunk of his car. Jean-Claude greeted him at the door.

"Oliver! So glad you could join us."

"You're both so kind to have me," he responded as he shook his host's hand firmly. He offered him the Shiraz.

"Ah," Jean-Claude beamed, "you've always had excellent taste in wines. I can't wait to try this." He beckoned Oliver inside. "Hanako is in town picking up a few essentials. Why don't you make yourself at home before dinner. You'll be staying in the downstairs bedroom just behind the staircase. There's a bathroom next door."

"Thanks."

It was more of a chateau than a cottage. Two storeys and four bedrooms, a broad, turning staircase at one end of the living room. The interior was predominantly pine, inspiring a warm, rustic feel. Yet, from what he could see, it was tastefully furnished with elegant modern amenities – bookshelves, a large-screen television, a stereo, a well-stocked bar, exquisite paintings and sculptures. Every well-appointed feature paid tribute to its owners' sophistication and taste.

Oliver stashed his bag in his bedroom and enjoyed a leisurely walk around the lake before dinner.

Dinner at Hanako and Jean-Claude's was always a sensuous experience. Jean-Claude prided himself as a gourmet and treated his guests to creative, sumptuous banquets. On this occasion, he opened the proceedings with a chestnut and truffle soup that was as artfully presented as it was delicious, paired with a crisp Rhineland Reisling. A Mozart string quartet set the mood over the stereo.

"You always make me feel inadequate, Jean-Claude," Oliver gushed. "You own a chain of stores and yet still manage to find the time to create the most exquisite meals I've ever enjoyed."

"Thanks. But if you love cooking good food – and especially *eating* it – it's not a big chore. Besides, Hanako doesn't like to cook anything fancy, so I have to do it myself if I want to eat well."

"Where do you get truffles?" Oliver asked, more out of politeness than genuine interest.

"Oh, if you know where to look, you can find anything," Jean-Claude began with great enthusiasm. "There are even some locally-grown Canadian truffles now. Apparently, the key is to cultivate a site with the appropriate trees and the right soil and climatic conditions, while keeping away competing fungi. But for a soup like this, a high-quality truffle oil is sufficient. In general, I get what I need from an épicerie in Outremont."

"So Oliver," Hanako interjected, drawing an icy glare from her husband, "how do you like this area? I don't think you've been to our cottage before."

"It's beautiful. The lake, the trees, the mountains. It's just perfect," he replied.

"If only there weren't so many moustiques," Jean-Claude groaned, fingering his sandy goatee.

"Mosquitos," Hanako corrected. Then to Oliver, "I hope it gives you some time to reflect."

Jean-Claude served the main course with great fanfare, in a painted earthenware pot with handles on each side. "This is my special take on boeuf borguignon, with a miso wine sauce and shiitake mushrooms. It has a unique 'East meets West' flavour, sort of like us," he said proudly, pointing at Hanako. "Your Shiraz should go nicely with it."

Oliver tasted it and declared it a coup de grace. They washed it down with liberal helpings of the wine, which put them all in more relaxed moods. After enjoying a rich mousse au chocolat for dessert, they retired to the living room sofa with a bottle of Armagnac, while Jean-Claude expounded on the Liberal Party's prospects in the next provincial election. Eventually, he tired of that subject and began quizzing Oliver on his business.

"So Oliver, you still have only one office?" It was more of an indictment than a question.

"Well, yes. It's a practice," Oliver replied, scratching his ear vigorously.

"Yeah, well, if you had more locations and hired more notaries, you could increase your volume. That's what I did with my optometry stores. There's an optometrist on site at each location, but they're salaried. The profits come to me."

"I do okay as it is. I don't need the hassle of running multiple offices." As usual, Oliver observed irritably, Hanako didn't talk much when the three of them met. Jean-Claude tended to run the show.

"How much is enough?" Jean-Claude had the temerity to ask. His wife coughed audibly.

"Jean-Claude! I'd prefer not to talk about money," Oliver replied a little too aggressively, no doubt because of the wine.

"We wouldn't be able to afford our house in the Plateau, this cottage and our pied-a-terre in the south of France if I had only one store. You could do something similar."

"It's something to think about," Oliver said through gritted, tobacco-stained teeth.

"Don't think too long, buddy. I don't want to mind your business, but__"

Hanako interrupted, "You must both be tired of talking business after a long week. I know *I* am. Why don't we play a game to unwind." With that, she pulled *Catan* off the shelf and they busied themselves building roads, settlements and cities. Jean-Claude won and touted his superior strategy, but they all agreed it was an excellent way to end their first evening together.

Saturday morning was a peerless weekend morning. By the time Oliver emerged for breakfast at ten-thirty, nary a cloud despoiled the deep azure sky and the golden sun graced each ripple of the idyllic forest lake with its manifold blessings. With the temperature expected to approach eighteen degrees, Hanako rejoiced that it would be warm enough for kayaking. Jean-Claude, who never learned to swim, graciously proposed that Oliver join Hanako at the lake for a bit, while he caught up on some reading. Oliver cheerfully agreed.

He followed Hanako to a shed whence they retrieved two kayaks – one tomato red, the other lime green, like the extremities of a giant traffic light – together with life jackets and paddles. These they dragged along the grass to the shoreline. Hanako, in her smart, geometric one-piece swimsuit, climbed into the lime kayak and started paddling to the middle of the lake, leaving Oliver to trail in the red.

He admired Hanako's swift, graceful strokes; his were more frenetic. He found it all hypnotic: the regular movement of her bronzed arms, the slop, slop of the paddle through the water, the tranquil breeze, the sun and trees reflected in the shimmering lake. For the first part of the afternoon, they said little, preferring to bask in the serenity, the solitude, their camaraderie of silence. Apart from a motorboat further afield and some bathers on the far shore, they had their section of the lake to themselves. For the first time since his brother's death, Oliver's soul was almost at peace.

After they rowed and drifted for some time, Hanako steered her craft over to his and stopped paddling. He followed suit.

"How are you doing?" she asked, her large, lustrous ebony eyes registering concern.

"Oh, it's great to be out here. This lake is gorgeous!" he replied.

"That's not what I meant." She studied his tired, wan face, the bloodshot eyes his sunglasses did little to conceal. "How are you holding up?"

"I'll be alright," he said. "If only I could sleep."

Hanako watched the water lap up against Oliver's kayak. The gentle bobbing of the boat, the freshness of the air, their solitude lent an intimacy to their conversation. "You didn't have an opportunity to say goodbye to Paul. That makes it harder," Hanako observed.

"I don't think it makes much difference," he demurred. "Death is death."

"Maybe," she said, nodding her head ever so slightly, her ponytail bobbing back and forth. "But Western culture fetishizes death too much. I was taught that death was a part of life. You have to make your peace with it. That would help you grieve properly, allow you to cry."

Oliver said nothing, retreating into his private thoughts.

Hanako recited softly, "Since the day of my birth, my death began its walk. It is walking toward me, without hurrying."

"What's that?" Oliver inquired. He waved away a mosquito that buzzed around his ear.

"An old Japanese saying. My father taught it to me when I was young."

"I like it," he said simply.

"Let's paddle out toward that bridge," she said, suddenly animated. "The trees there are magnificent."

The lake was long and meandering. The section on which Hanako and Jean-Claude's cottage stood was quite wide, but it narrowed to the east, where a time-worn, red-brick pedestrian bridge spanned a constricted channel that opened into a forested basin. They propelled themselves under the bridge into what Hanako called the prettier part of the lake. Once there, they circled the contours of that section, enjoying the dense surrounding forest, its vibrant spring foliage.

With fewer cottages on this part of the lake, they felt secluded from the eyes of the world. Capitalizing on their splendid isolation, Hanako paddled to the middle and began singing a Japanese song softly. Oliver sat mesmerized by her honeyed voice, the strangeness to his ear of the foreign lyrics, the beauty of the forest, the allure of Hanako's singular personality. "That was wonderful," he gushed when she finished singing. "What was it?"

She smiled. "A popular song about the flower of a dogwood tree. I probably messed up some of the words. I'm afraid I don't speak Japanese very well."

"Please sing something else," he entreated. "You sing beautifully."

She sang another song, with Oliver's every sense strained toward her. When she finished, the friends lapsed into silence.

Hanako seemed lost in thought, staring up at the vast expanse of the sky. She turned her head slowly toward him and said with forced nonchalance, "Oliver, we've been friends for a long time. Can I ask you something?"

"Of course," he answered.

"Do you remember when we met, all those years ago?"

"At the Jazz Festival, sure.... I think it was the Jeff Healey show, with his Jazz Hounds band."

"Jazz Wizards," Hanako corrected.

"That's right. And then we ran into each other again at Liz Hanley's party not long afterward."

Hanako swallowed hard. "In all that time, why did you never ask me out or make a pass at me?"

The boat shook. The lake itself trembled. Oliver's pulse raced. *What did she ask?* His whole body tensed. He felt a gnawing at the pit of his stomach. He had to master his emotions before speaking. "I did… I mean, I wanted to. You can't imagine how *much* I wanted to. More than anything in the world…. But I was afraid… of ruining our friendship. And then you started seeing Jean-Claude and it was too late." He didn't say, *Because I was intimidated by you, in awe of you. Because I thought I wasn't good enough for you. That you could never love someone like me.*

"Oh…." she said softly, "I always thought it was because you didn't like me that way. Maybe that you weren't attracted to me."

"Oh God! That's not at all…."

His canoe was veering toward a patch of water lilies, so he paddled to the right to avoid them. He mused, still reeling from her question, its implications, "When I was in high school, I was really close friends with a girl. I used to speak to her for hours several nights a week. God, I held a torch for her…. When I *finally* worked up the courage to ask her out__"

"Yes. You told me about her. Marie."

Oliver nodded severely. "She made some *lame* excuse why she couldn't and that was the end of our friendship. After that, she never seemed to have time to talk anymore. I guess I was afraid that would happen with *you*, too," he explained, absently scratching the hull of the boat with his nail.

They paddled together silently for a while, each nursing their own wounds, as the sun sank lower toward the horizon.

"I never realized just how much she scarred me," he said at last.

"Well, you can't really blame her. She was young and she got spooked. She didn't know how to handle it."

"Maybe. But it still really hurt."

A small, low-flying plane traversed overhead, disrupting the peace with its mechanical whirring.

"Paul always told me I was too sensitive. He thought I dwelled on Marie, mooned over her really, for far too long," he recalled wistfully. "You know, that's a funny thing. We were physically identical, but we were so different in many intangible ways. *Paul* was the one that was comfortable with women… knew how to behave with them, not me. Women couldn't keep their hands off him. With me… well, they always wanted to be friends, never anything more. I was really jealous of him sometimes."

"I was thinking," Hanako began, apparently trying to steer the conversation back to safer ground, "why don't you compose a poem to commemorate Paul? It might help to bring you peace."

"A poem?"

"Yes. Nothing fancy, just a couple of lines. There's a Japanese tradition of writing death haikus to mourn a loved one. You could try it, too," she suggested.

He mulled the idea over for a bit. Then he inquired, "Are there rules to writing one?"

"I don't know."

"Well, are there... you know, a certain number of lines? Does it have to rhyme?" he pressed.

"Look. I really don't know. You have to understand: I'm not really Japanese," she declared, her voice rising, her shoulders suddenly tensing.

"What do you mean?"

"It's just.... Everyone wants me to be an avatar of Japanese culture. I do too, in a way. But I was raised here and am more Canadian than Japanese. My mother raised me to forget the past. To assimilate. I remember some stuff my father taught me, but that's about it. Now that he's gone, I'm trying to learn more, to reconnect to my Japanese heritage. But in truth I don't know very much. It makes me feel a fraud."

He was moved by her frankness. "Okay," he said. "I'll give it a go. Let me think about it," he said.

"You could probably read about death haiku's online and see some examples, if you want. But you don't have to follow any rules. I'm just trying to find a way to help you express your feelings toward Paul and mourn his loss."

He watched a group of children trailing a kite in a clearing on the shore. It was flying too high, near the trees. He feared it would get caught. He was about to try to warn them, when it suddenly occurred to him to ask, his heart aflutter, his stomach back in his mouth, "Hanako.... Did you want me to? ... Ask you out, I mean."

She stared past him stoically, her soft pink lips contorted, curving downward toward a mole on her chin, lost in thought. Eventually she said, "It's getting late. We've been out all afternoon. Let's head back to get ready for dinner." With that, she resumed her rhythmic paddling, and pulled away from him toward the shore.

For dinner, Oliver invited his hosts to a chic "resto-pub" in Saint-Sauveur. From the get-go, Jean-Claude was in an irritable mood, which became more frayed as the night unfolded. They arrived on time for their eight o'clock reservation, but were made to wait twenty minutes to be seated. It then took a while to get the server's attention. The sommelier recommended what Oliver judged to be a superb Bordeaux, but Jean-Claude complained that it was too acid. He found fault, too, with his foie gras appetizer, which he derided as too heavy.

Hanako, her right hand supporting her chin, the frosted tips of her fingers tightly pressed against her cheek, attempted to cover for her husband with small talk while they waited for their main course to arrive. "I just love the décor and the presentation here. It's very artistic," she said with forced brightness.

"Hah! Spoken like a graphic artist, rather than a gourmande," her husband countered condescendingly.

"Well, I *am* a graphic artist, dear! Is that a problem?" she snapped uncharacteristically.

"I don't know," Oliver offered, eager to defuse tensions. "I also find the atmosphere and presentation charming. Hopefully, the main course will be to your liking, Jean-Claude."

"Don't get me wrong, Oliver. You chose this place and it *is* one I wanted to try also. I think they're just off their game to-night." Even when Jean-Claude tried to be diplomatic, he seemed to pour more fuel on the fire. Hanako squeezed his thigh under the table in the hope of restraining him, but he glared at her angrily through the rectangular lenses of his spectacles.

The waiter arrived with their main courses: flank steak served on a wooden board with vegetables and gratin dauphinois for Oliver, glazed duck breast with polenta for Hanako, and Swordfish Carpaccio for Jean-Claude.

As Hanako watched nervously, Jean-Claude sampled his meal and, with a slight nod of his goatee, signified his approval. It appeared that the storm had passed. When Oliver cut into his steak, however, Jean-Claude was offended.

"They overcooked it!" he practically shouted.

"No, it's not that bad," Oliver dissented, hoping to avoid a scene. His right hand reached unconsciously for his ear, which he rubbed slowly.

"You've got to stand up for yourself, Oliver. A place like this shouldn't overcook their steaks. Look. It's shoe leather! You don't pay forty-five dollars for that." He signalled for the waiter.

"Oui Monsieur?" the waiter inquired.

"Le monsieur a commandé une bavette à point, mais elle est trop cuite!" Jean-Claude complained.

"Vraiment?" The waiter examined Oliver's steak. "À mon avis, elle est assez rouge."

"Moi, je dit que c'est trop cuite! Imbecile!"

Annoyed, the waiter agreed to bring Oliver another steak. Jean-Claude continued to heap abuse on him after he left the table, saying that even an amateur could spot an overcooked steak. And what kind of chef couldn't cook a proper steak? Oliver couldn't understand what had gotten into Jean-Claude and found his behaviour embarrassing. Mortified, Hanako said she felt unwell and insisted on returning to the cottage after the main course, without ordering dessert.

They said little on the ride back. When they arrived, Oliver announced that he would have a smoke outside and take a walk around the lake. His promenade lasted over an hour, as he tried to make sense of the day's perplexing events. Upon his return, his hosts were still arguing loudly in their bedroom upstairs, so he turned in early, grateful to avoid another confrontation with Jean-Claude.

That night, Oliver was too agitated to sleep. He kept replaying the kayak adventure he had with Hanako, their conversation, in his mind. What did it all mean? What was she saying to him? And why had Jean-Claude been uncharacteristically aggressive this evening? He was unable to settle down, so after tossing and turning for a while – his usual nighttime regimen of late – he repaired to the kitchen for a 3 AM drink.

To his surprise, he found the kitchen light on. Hanako was perched atop a wooden stool at the breakfast bar with a cup of tea, wearing a revealing cream silk nighty. Her olive cheeks flushed as he entered. His heart aflutter, he apologized awkwardly for intruding and turned to leave.

"No, it's okay," she said quickly. "I just didn't expect you…. One of Jean-Claude's stores was broken into. The police called and he had to drive back to Montreal. He should be back by morning. In all the excitement, I couldn't sleep."

She made no move to cover up. He could see her charming neck and shapely bare arms, the contours of her breasts and stomach through the almost translucent silk, the full expanse of her slender legs to the top of her thighs. Completely flustered, he was unsure whether to remain in the kitchen or retreat to his room.

"Neither could I," he muttered uncomfortably, averting his gaze from her.

"Still the coffin?"

"Yes," he lied.

Hanako asked shily, "Do you want something to drink? Can I get you something?" She too seemed uncertain, hesitant.

"No…. Well, I mean… I was going to see if I could find some port or whiskey to help me sleep. But I don't want to disturb you."

She motioned to another stool and bade him sit while she retreated to the liquor cabinet in what served as the cottage's dining room. She returned with two shot glasses and a decanter of amber liquid. "Will sherry do?" she asked. Still no effort to cover herself.

"Uh-huh," Oliver assented uneasily.

She filled two glasses and sat down beside him. As she leaned over to pour, he caught sight of the top of her breasts below the plunging neckline. A shiver went down his spine. He tried to hide his arousal with forced banter.

"Nothing like some sherry to calm one's nerves in the middle of the night," he said absurdly, taking a long sip.

"Why do you think you always see his coffin being lowered into the grave?" she asked. "Why is it never his face – your face – lying in the coffin? Or the undertaker shovelling dirt on it?" She crossed her legs and all he could think of was her beautiful knees, her athletic thighs, and what was hiding just above, behind the flimsy lingerie.

"I don't know," he murmured dizzily, almost breathlessly.

"Oh, sorry," she said, noticing his agitation. "I thought you wanted to talk about it."

"I don't know.... Maybe I should let you go back to sleep."

"No!" she said, too quickly. "I mean... I'm not likely to fall asleep again now. And you *never* sleep nowadays. So why don't we just go into the living room and put some music on?" she suggested.

"Okay."

Once in the living room, Hanako refilled their sherry glasses and sat on one side of the off-white twill sofa, again crossing her legs. She pointed to the far shelf, next to the television, ordering him to "See if you can find something in our CD collection that speaks to you."

"Wow! I see the seventies are alive and well here," he exclaimed in mock alarm, as he rummaged through two large wicker baskets full of discs. Eventually, he selected the Chocolate Bullfrogs' *Startstruck* album and the Rolling Stones Live at the Marquee Club. He inserted the former into the CD player.

As the music began to play, Hanako took a swig from her glass and cooed, "Oh! Let's dance!"

He complied, gently heaving her up by the hand and leading her to the carpeted space in front of the television. At first, they danced nervously and uncomfortably, with Oliver too conscious of the movement of her legs, the criss-cross silk straps across her open back when she twirled, the touch of her fingers. As the sherry did its work, the Chocolate Bullfrogs' lyrics – *Damnation's my lot, that I can tell, but with you I can brave the fires of Hell* – seemed to speak directly to them, loosening them up, intensifying their bond.

When the first CD ended, they returned to the sofa laughing. She reached over and adjusted the part in his bushy almond hair, again revealing the upper limits of her breasts.

"Why don't you part it to the right?" she inquired freely. "It makes you look even better."

He ignored her question. "I had an *amazing* time on the lake today. I could have stayed there with you *forever*."

"Yes," she agreed. "There's nothing in the *world* like being out in a kayak on a day like today." Suddenly, she fixed him with a darker, penetrating expression. "You've never liked Jean-Claude much, have you?"

He started to protest, "That's not true. He's a great guy," but the stern look in her eyes seemed to say 'We've been closer than any friends have been for so long. Don't lie to me!' So he took another sip of sherry and answered earnestly, "No, I suppose I never have."

She took a breath and was about to react, but then fell silent, playing absently with a zipper on a sofa cushion.

"Why do you stay with him?" He would have asked why she married him in the first place, but now feared he knew the answer.

She looked away from him, toward a Sabina painting of autumn leaves above the fireplace, a haunting premonition of how the optimistic May blossoms around the lake outside would meet their end, a testament to the ephemeral nature of life. "He's good to me," she said without conviction.

Oliver sighed, sensing for the first time Hanako's inner misery and loneliness. It had never occurred to him that she, who was so wise and giving, who to all appearances had the model marriage, could feel so lost.

"Do you...." He hesitated, his voice almost hoarse. "Do you love him, Hanako?"

She turned her head slowly and stared deeply into his tired, caramel eyes, probing his soul. She opened her mouth as if to answer, but then shut it again. After an interval, it was her turn to stand and pull him to the dance floor.

"Let's put on another disc and dance some more."

Oliver cued up the Rolling Stones album and, with the softer, bluesy music, began dancing slowly, closely. He held her tightly, his face brushing hers, the swell of her bosom pressing against his chest, his hands caressing the soft exposed skin of her back. He was overcome by emotion, inwardly cursing his paralysis, the agony he had brought upon himself, the bitter harvest of friend-ship that was his consolation prize.

Hanako abandoned herself to his embrace, playing with his hair, gently kissing his stubbly cheek. She, too, seemed to revel in a desire long suppressed, a desperate hope too long denied, a too-long repressed dream of happiness about to be fulfilled. But something in the melancholy moan of the heart-rending saxo-phone solo on *I Got the Blues* shook her. Tears streamed down her face. She shook her head. Her whole body began to shiver. Without an explanation or apology, she pulled herself from his grasp and ran upstairs to her bedroom, leaving Oliver bewildered and guilt-ridden in her wake.

Oliver emerged early the following morning, all packed and prepared to depart. He found Jean-Claude in the kitchen.

"Morning, Oliver. What a night!" Jean-Claude's gaze fell upon Oliver's overnight bag. "You leaving? I thought you were staying until tomorrow."

"Something came up," Oliver said. "I have a real estate deal closing tomorrow which just got moved up to the morning instead of the afternoon. I need to get back to the office and handle the preparations today."

"That's too bad. I was hoping to spend some time with you today. How much is a deal like that worth?"

"Oh, not much," he replied coldly, to his host's disappointment. "It's a small storefront on Avenue du Parc. Probably worth only about three hundred thousand or so."

"I see. And how much do you make from something like that, if you don't mind my asking," Jean-Claude pressed.

"After expenses, only about a thousand."

"It's a shame you have to go back for just that, but I guess it can't be avoided," Hanako's husband observed. "Do you want me to wake Hanako before you go?"

"No, let her sleep," he said, a little too quickly. "And please give her this. It's my death haiku for Paul. I wrote it last night." Oliver handed him a used envelope with two scribbled lines on the back. It read *Grander half in all facets of life. Your premature parting casts my soul adrift.* It could easily have applied to Hanako.

Jean-Claude shot him a quizzical look.

"What happened at the store last night?" Oliver queried.

"A typical smash and grab. Coffee?"

Oliver nodded. His host filled a kettle and ignited the gas stove. It seemed incongruous to Oliver that someone of Jean-Claude's culinary sensibilities used instant coffee.

"The front window was smashed with a crowbar or something. They didn't get much from the register, but they looted the display cases. I don't know what they'll be able to do with a bunch of glasses frames," Jean-Claude said. "You like it black, right?"

"Yes, thanks. Did you get any sleep?"

"About an hour. You want some eggs? I make a mean omelette," his host offered.

"No, thanks. I should really hit the road. I love it here, but the sooner I get back, the sooner I can stop worrying about the transaction." Oliver threw back his coffee and stood to leave. Jean-Claude accompanied him to his car.

"Please thank Hanako for me. You guys have been great. I really appreciate it."

Jean-Claude responded curiously. "Thank *you*, Oliver."

"Me? For what?"

Jean-Claude stared stone-faced at the ground, his goatee pressed to his chest, and said quietly, "For doing the decent thing." His words sent a chill down Oliver's spine. *How much did he know?*

Oliver climbed behind the wheel and started off for Montreal.

He drove distractedly along the dirt road leading from the lake, oblivious of the splendour of the forest in the early morning mist. His head was bursting, his life in disarray. *Why is it,* he wondered bitterly, *that no matter how great our triumphs, it is our failures that define us?* His thoughts turned to Hanako. She had saved herself from disaster and disgrace. But at what cost? *Why must we sacrifice what we hold dearest to remain true to ourselves? Perhaps that's what love is,* he reflected acidly. *Love is sacrifice. You don't truly love what you're unwilling to renounce for its own sake.* At the traffic light, he turned onto the regional route that leads to the highway.

Life without. That's what death was. Life without Paul. His compass. His north star. Life without Hanako. His sun, his moon, his entire galaxy. Not light as a feather, he decided, but bleak as eternity.

Distracted as he was, he noticed a doe crossing the road far too late. Instinctively, he jerked the car off the road to avoid the animal, braking hard to stop the vehicle just before it hit a tree. The near miss caused his hands to shake, his whole body to heave. As he sat on the dirt and pebble shoulder, at long last the tears began to flow from his eyes, from his heart, from the very core of his wounded soul. He cried for his brother, his twin, his better self. For Hanako, the greatest gift in his life, whose friendship must now end for her sake. For all the lost opportunities of his life. For the night that would live forever in his mind, to his everlasting shame and torment.

The Satchel

"You Mr. Phillips?" Bill called out the window to the man in the brown leather bomber jacket and tan pants emerging from the Lord Nelson Hotel.

"Yup," the man replied as he approached the vehicle. He scrutinized his driver critically, noting his white hair and moustache, his rectangular, metal-framed spectacles, the creased navy jacket with the red Atlantic Limousine insignia.

"I'm Bill. Nice to meet you. Do ya want me to put that in the trunk?" Bill asked. Phillips shook his head and clambered into the back seat, placing his large grey knapsack gingerly on the floor. Bill switched off the radio as the Melancholy Grapes were crooning, '*just another empty night on the boulevard....*'

The limousine pulled out of the taxi rank and threaded through the city streets, as Phillips checked his cell phone. "You flying Air Canada?" Bill asked. The passenger grunted his assent.

At the first stoplight, Bill used his handsfree device to call the office. "Passenger Phillips in car. Headed to the airport," was all he said before disconnecting. He took the measure of his client through the rear-view mirror: a pale-faced man in his forties, of medium height and build, with a rather obvious and awkward toupee. "Where you from?" he inquired affably.

"Ontario," came the reticent reply.

Eager to start a conversation, Bill gave it another try. "What do you do there?" he persisted. With his right hand, he reached into a cooler on the passenger seat and fished out a plastic cola bottle, which he twisted open and took a draft from before placing it in the cup holder.

"I'm a contractor," Phillips replied in a tone that suggested he'd rather be left alone.

Alright, Bill concluded resignedly, one hand on the apex of the steering wheel, the other fingering his bushy white moustache dolefully. *I'll have to do all the talking on this run.*

"Me, I used to be in the Navy, but I've been landlocked and driving this limo for over twenty years now. Not as exciting, but you'd be surprised. This line of work is a lot more interesting than you'd think," Bill said amiably, as the cab approached the McDonald Bridge. "I could tell you hundreds of stories about the people who rode in my car."

From the centre point of the bridge, his passenger took in the expansive view of the harbour, the downtown, Dartmouth on the other side of the water. The early evening sky was darkening, and it was typical, moody Halifax weather, so visibility was limited. But the vista still commanded his attention.

"In fact, you'll never believe what happened to me just this morning," Bill volunteered. "It was most curious and mighty terrifying!" Without responding, Phillips stared at Bill expectantly through the rear-view mirror, his curiosity piqued.

"I usually work the night shift. I'm just starting now. You're my first fare of the night. All night long, it's from the city to the airport and back, again and again. Not that I'm complaining or anything. It suits my temperament, and I got nothing else to do with my nights…. Anyway, early this morning, my last trip before calling it a night was a pick-up at the airport, a businessman in a fancy suit, wearing shoes that cost more than my cab, I'll wager. But he looked like one tough piece of work. Had a boxer's build, he did. He smiled an' all and was friendly as can be to me. But I could tell that you wouldn't want to cross him. I know it sounds silly, but there was a nastiness in the way he held his jaw." After traversing the centre of Dartmouth, the car turned right onto the 118.

"He was flyin' in from Vancouver, he said. Had lots of luggage for just one person. Two big suitcases and a garment bag, which he put into the trunk. It was real odd that he put 'em in himself. Wouldn't let me touch them, even though the bags looked real heavy." Bill paused to change lanes and pass an SUV that was slowing down traffic. "Bloody Sunday driver!" he complained, as they reached the shiny blue expanse of Lake Charles on the right, still gleaming dreamily in the waning daylight.

"But he had this big, brown, bulging satchel – sort of the same colour as your jacket, my friend, but a little lighter – that he wouldn't put in the trunk. Just kept it with him, he did, right next to him throughout the ride. I could swear he had his hand on it the whole time, like he was afraid someone'd grab it from him. I tried to make conversation during the ride. You know, I'm a little chatty, especially since my Mabel passed on. I hope it doesn't disturb you, but it's the best way to pass the time when you're driving all night…"

"Not at all," Phillips muttered graciously to the mirror, urging Bill to continue with his eyes.

"It's funny. My Mabel always told me, 'Billy, you talk too much. One day you're gonna get yourself in a mess o' trouble,'" Bill said with a nostalgic laugh. "Well, he was polite, but our boy wasn't in a talking mood. Just kept texting with his phone. Every few seconds, PING! He got another text and kept firing his own back, fingers flyin' at the speed of sound. I thought it must be some girlfriend or wife or somethin'. Anyway, just as we were pulling up to where he lives, in one of them fancy Brunswick Street apartments, he gets a call and starts whispering, all agitated like. So I get out to open the trunk and help him with his bags and again he wouldn't let me get near 'em. There he is, the phone pressed against his ear with his shoulder as he's lifting out the heavy cases one by one with the other hand and waving me away. He even dropped the phone once and swore like a sailor. Then he comes round to the front, reaches into his wallet and stuffs five twenties in my hand and walks away without asking for change, still talking on the phone. Kept saying something like, 'don't worry, I took care of it.'"

"Took care of what?" the passenger asked, with growing interest.

"Oh, your guess is as good as mine. I try to mind my own business when my customers are on the phone. I'm not a busy-body, you know." Phillips adjusted his toupee and beamed a knowing smile.

"Anyway," Bill continued, glad to have reached his passenger, to have connected to someone in his loneliness, at least for the space of the ride, "in all the excitement of the phone call, getting his luggage and paying for the ride, he forgot all about his precious satchel on the seat. Just plumb forgot. I didn't notice myself and headed home to plop into bed after a long night.

When I pulled into the driveway, I look in the mirror for some reason, and that's when I saw it, sitting pretty there just like the Taj Mahal. Just then the call came over the radio from dispatch. Said that my last fare, on Brunswick, left his bag in the car. Could I bring it to him right away. I said I was beat and asked if I could swing it by in the afternoon. Not as young as I used to be, you know. They checked with him, then told me he couldn't wait. I had to drop it off right away."

The car merged onto highway 102 as night descended, shrouding the surrounding lakes and forests in a misty darkness. A loud ping signalled that Phillips had received a text on his phone. After consulting it, he announced, "It looks like my buddy will be arriving by car and wants me to meet him in the parking lot. Can you drop me off there, rather than the terminal?"

"No problem," Bill assured him. "So, staring at the satchel, I was mighty intrigued. It looked like it was fit to burst. I wondered, what could our boy *have* in there? What was so important that he had to have it *now*, at five-thirty in the AM?" He paused for effect, enjoying his passenger's rapt attention in the mirror.

"But then I thought, 'No, Billy boy. It ain't none of your business.' So I turned the key in the engine and started off again."

"So you didn't look inside?" Phillips asked in disappointment.

"Well, no," Bill replied, switching on his brights on the largely empty highway. "Not right away, anyway. But then, as I was driving, I kept wondering and wondering, 'what's he got in there?' I don't know.... Something just didn't feel right. After a few blocks, curiosity got the better of me – it was eating away at me – and I pulled over to the side of the road. I climbed into the back and examined the bag under the cabin light. It looked rather ordinary. No lock or anything. And I thought, 'oh it can't be anything too important or he'd have a lock on it.' But it also meant that I could just take a wee peek without him knowing anything about it. And you couldn't really blame me. It was *his* fault for leaving it in the car, after all…"

"So what was inside?" Phillips pressed excitedly.

"Ah," Bill said, again fingering his moustache, shivering slightly. "It was quite a shock. A *horrible* shock. I unlatched the case, and you'll never believe what I saw…" He paused again for dramatic effect. "It was overflowing with one-hundred-dollar bills! There must've been over half a million dollars in the case! I've never seen so much money." The passenger whistled.

"But that was only the appetizer. If only that was all…. As I was staring at all that cash, dumbfounded, I noticed the top edge of a plastic bag sticking out. You know, the Ziplock bags you get in grocery stores?" The man in the mirror nodded. "Well, I pulled it out and you'll never guess what was inside."

"What?" Phillips demanded impatiently, his whole body leaning forward.

"It was *horrible*! Just horrible." Another pause, as Bill swallowed hard. "There were…. There were five severed, bloody fingers in the bag!" Bill shuddered. "In that light, I couldn't tell if they were from the same hand and, to be honest, I didn't much care. I was so rattled, I shoved everything back in the satchel and quickly snapped the clasp shut. I figured this guy must be mixed up in drugs or organized crime or something like that and I'd be better off having nothing to do with it. Only I was so shaken that I pushed too hard and broke the clasp, so it didn't close fully! Man, was I scared!" A light rain began to fall. Bill engaged the windshield wipers on the intermittent setting.

"I didn't know what to do. If he saw the latch and knew that I peeked inside, I could be a goner. But if I didn't return it, I was most definitely toast," Bill explained. "I was terrified!"

A little agitated by the memory, Bill paused to drink a little more of his cola. He opened his window a crack to let in some of the damp, forest air. After a breath or two, he resumed his tale.

"In a near panic, I tried as best as I could to hide the damage and drove back to our boy's apartment. I rang from below and asked him to come down to pick up his bag, but he insisted that I bring it up. I thought I was safer in the lobby, with people around, but was too afraid to argue. You know, when you're scared, you sometimes don't think too clearly. So, I went upstairs. Well, this boy has the fanciest penthouse suite you've ever seen. All the luxuries and the most beautiful view of the Citadel. So, my buddy shakes my hand and welcomes me in with the friendliest smile. But I got to tell you, it gave me the willies. I don't know. Maybe it was just my imagination, but I thought I saw a menacing edge to that smile, and it chilled me to the bone," Bill confided.

"So I hand over the case and he thanks me. But then he asks me rather casually, 'You didn't open it by any chance, did you?' Well, all the blood drained out of my face, and I quickly answered no. I hadn't. That's when he looks down at the case and sees the damaged clasp. I could *see* him noticing it, see the wheels turning in his head. My stomach started churning. I've never been so scared. Even in the worst days in Bosnia in the 90s, I was never that scared. Then he reached into the breast pocket of his jacket and I nearly fainted, 'cause I was certain he was pulling out a gun. I just *knew* I was going to join my Mabel. But he just pulled out a fifty and offered it to me as sweet as cherry pie. 'Thanks, Bill,' he said. 'I'm lucky I had an honest driver like you.' You could've bowled me over with a feather!" Bill's phone rang. Glancing at the dashboard, he saw that it was dispatch, but he decided to ignore it for the time being. He'd call back in a few minutes, after dropping his passenger off at the airport.

"Sweating profusely," he continued, "I nodded my appreciation – I could hardly speak I was so frightened – and hightailed it out of there as fast as I could. I was almost hyperventilating all the way down the elevator. It felt like my chest would explode. But I got out safe and sound. When I got back home it took a couple of scotches to settle me down so I could sleep. But here I am now, good as new." Reaching the airport exit, Bill steered the vehicle off the highway and glided past the nearby Tim Horton's.

"That's quite a story!" exclaimed the passenger. "Did you call the police?"

"No," Bill said, as he followed the green sign into the airport's parking lot. "Of course, I thought of it. But a driver's got to respect the confidentiality of his clients, you know. Besides, those fingers really rattled me. I thought, 'This guy's not someone to be trifled with. Let someone else turn him in.'"

He glided to a stop under a streetlamp, instinctively inspecting the gas gauge in its dismal light, as he did at the end of each trip. A quarter of a tank left. He'd have to refill it before the next pick-up. He suppressed a sigh, disappointed that the ride, the conversation was over. *Oh well, perhaps the next pick-up'll be more talkative.* Still, he had managed to reach the man after all, so it wasn't all bad.

Putting the car into park, Bill glanced into the mirror to see his interlocutor's reaction to his tale, to cement the common bond he had forged during the ride, only to find himself staring down the barrel of a Beretta, fitted with a silencer. The man looked almost apologetic as the gun trembled slightly, emitting an audible PFFFT. Bill slumped back into his seat as Mr. Phillips exited the vehicle and jumped into a waiting car in the drizzly Nova Scotia night.

Special Delivery

It started as an ordinary, run-of-the-mill day in the delivery room of a hospital in downtown Montreal. Aline, the mother-to-be, was reclining on her back, her legs spread apart, her face all red and contorted, shrieking like a banshee. Dr. Fernandez, the intern, was elbow-deep in her body cavity frantically searching for the baby's head. Sandrine, the veteran nurse, was passing her utensils with tears in her eyes, like she always had during live births, repeating "what a miracle, what a miracle," as if this were the first birth she had ever witnessed. Father-to-be Fred was wearing a hole in the carpet with his nervous pacing, muttering "I'm too young to be a father" under his breath. And, to cap the scene, Dr. Bertrand, the obstetrician, stood aloof from the action wearing a beatific smile upon his chapped lips, doing not much of anything at all. Yes, it was a typical childbirth.

Suddenly, Dr. Fernandez shouted, "I see it!" causing Sandrine to cross herself and recite "Praised be God!" and Fred to faint, collapsing like a sandcastle into the standard issue hospital chair.

After some intense pushing, the occasional cuss word from Aline, and prompts from Dr. Fernandez for her to breathe like she was taught in Lamaze class, the drama was brought to its conclusion. Dr. Fernandez swaddled the newborn into a bundle of blankets and handed it to Dr. Bertrand, who had the honour of presenting it to the mother.

"Congratulations!" he boomed, "Meet the new addition to your family. It's a girl!"

Aline propped herself up on her elbows, sweat pouring down her face and hair, looking like the loser of a boxing match, and peered excitedly into the blankets. "It's..." she said in bewilderment, "it's a cell phone!"

"Yes," beamed Dr. Bertrand, "isn't she beautiful?"

At that moment, Fred recovered consciousness and stumbled over to the bed to meet his daughter. "B...but..." he objected, "weren't we supposed to have a baby?"

Dr. Bertrand threw Dr. Fernandez a knowing glance, as if to say 'we medical professionals have to deal with this kind of ignorant question from the uneducated all the time, but we must have forbearance.' "Apparently not, Mr. Butterfat," he responded patiently. "You are the proud parents of a beautiful little cell phone."

The nurse quickly took the newborn to the sunlamp to plug in her power cable and boot up her operating system. She then turned to the parents to ask, "What passcode would you like me to set for her?"

"I don't know," Aline replied slowly. "I didn't know I'd need one. What room number are we in?"

"2713," Sandrine supplied.

"Perfect! Let's go with that."

"But Doctor!" Fred interjected. "This is all kind of a shock for us. We had our hearts set on a baby, you see. I mean a *real* baby." Drs. Bertrand and Fernandez stared at him blankly. "Does uh… Does this kind of thing happen often?"

Once again, Dr. Bertrand fixed Dr. Fernandez with a 'You see what we have to deal with?" look. "Oh, sure. You never can be sure what will happen with a delivery. One time a woman delivered a fax machine! Genetics is very hard to predict. Isn't that right Dr. Fernandez?"

Not wanting to displease her supervisor, Dr. Fernandez responded quickly, "Yes, of course, Doctor. The important thing is to be happy with what you've got."

Neither Aline nor Fred appeared to be persuaded, but Dr. Bertrand merely shook their hands to congratulate them and shuffled off to officiate over another miracle of birth in a different delivery room. Sandrine advised Aline to rest while she took Fred and his new daughter to the post-natal room to weigh the newborn and fill out the required paperwork.

As the nurse was monitoring his daughter's vital statistics, Fred looked around at all the other babies in the post-natal room with envy. They were all good-looking, human babies. "How come mine's the only one that doesn't look like a normal baby?" he asked.

"Oh, you mean these? These are the Caesarian babies. They always look like movie stars because they don't get their heads battered and flattened as they push through the birth canal. You see how flat your daughter's head is?" She pointed to his daughter's screen. "But don't worry. It'll fill out in no time, and you won't be able to tell the difference between her and them in a few days."

Fred looked at her quizzically. "But she's a cell phone…"

"Oh, sure she's different," the nurse acknowledged. "But you have to respect her differences. Different is good!" Fred quickly and heartily agreed with her, so as not to be considered judgemental. In his heart of hearts, however, he longed for a baby that was like the others.

After completing the paperwork, Sandrine brought Fred and his daughter to a private room where the Butterfats could be alone with their newborn for the first time. As they gazed into her unfocused screen, they both felt immense disappointment. Aline moreover, was embarrassed and couldn't look Fred in the eye. *I guess I was spending too much time on my devices rather than with Fred*, she thought. *I even visited the odd compromising website. And now, the baby looks more like my laptop than like Fred. Oh, I'm so ashamed!!*

As if reading his wife's thoughts, Fred observed, "She doesn't look like my side of the family at all."

"Nonsense," Aline retorted guiltily. "Your Aunt Edna was square-jawed. And didn't you always say that your cousin Henry is a blockhead?"

"I suppose," he said dubiously.

"She'll be so different from all the other kids in her school when she grows up," Aline mused. "It's going to be a challenge. I'm not sure what she'll be able to contribute to her soccer team."

"Well, maybe she'll join the photography club instead," Fred offered optimistically.

"And what will we say to all our friends?" Aline continued, ignoring her husband's intervention. "Oh, it's so embarrassing!"

"Yes," Fred agreed sadly. "I wish we had normal child."

Their melancholy reverie was interrupted by a nurse, who came to teach them how to care for their little one.

"It's very important to hold her properly. They're very sensitive at this early stage. Be certain to wash your hands carefully before picking her up, and hold her gingerly by her edges. You don't want to smudge her screen," the nurse advised.

Aline nodded, while Fred retrieved a pen and paper to record all her advice.

She handed them a box of anti-static wipes. "They're very messy at this age, so you'll need to wipe her screen often."

"How often?" Fred queried.

The nurse thought for a moment before replying, "Raising children isn't an exact science. Just wipe her when it seems necessary."

"Got it," Fred assured her.

"Most importantly, you've got to feed your little one regularly." She handed Aline a charging cable and showed her how to insert it in their daughter's jack. "She'll let you know when she's hungry, but if you don't feed her enough, she'll end up sleeping. If you systematically underfeed her, then you could have real problems. So please be careful!"

"Thank you for all your help. We really appreciate it," Aline declared warmly.

"One final thing," the nurse said. "We need to register the birth. Have you decided what you're going to name her?"

"Well," ventured Fred, "I was thinking of naming her Nokia, after her grandfather."

"Oh, Fred dear!" Aline swooned, tears gathering around her bloodshot eyes. "Daddy would have been so proud!"

"Nokia it is!" Fred confirmed.

"Okay! Nokia Butterfat," the nurse recorded. "Enjoy your new daughter!"

The first few weeks were exhausting and trying. To begin with, there were the sleepless nights. Every few hours, the Butterfats' sleep would be shattered by the piercing ring of Nokia's little alarm, indicating that it was time to feed their precious bundle of joy. Fred took the late-night feedings, while Aline attended to her in the morning. But once they plugged her in, she rarely let them settle back to sleep. Instead, she would want to be entertained with sports scores, weather updates, and sometimes music. When they returned to bed, completely drained, they would inevitably disturb their partner. In this manner, they each slept no more than about four hours a night, which left them perpetually tired and irritable.

Eventually, as Nokia grew and her parents gained experience, they learned to minimize the nighttime disruption. A CLSC nurse who visited them a week after the birth explained how to set Nokia's alarm at regular intervals and replace it with a more soothing cricket sound to make feedings more routine and manageable. Fred even found a longer-life battery online that helped reduce the number of feedings per night.

Despite this progress, Fred and Aline still felt cheated. They wished Nokia were like all the other babies, making cooing sounds, rolling over and filling diapers. They wondered what they had done to be cursed with such an unusual child. The attitudes of family, friends and people they encountered in the street only reinforced their frustration.

One day, as they paraded Nokia through the neighbourhood in her carriage, they were dismayed by the reactions they got. "Hey lady," a well-meaning teenager volunteered, "I think you forgot your baby!" A man with more sinister motives snickered, "that baby is a little two-dimensional, just like its parents."

A conversation with Aline's elderly mother was emblematic of their family's reaction. "*This* is the grandchild you brought me? A cell phone?" she accused them.

"Mom, don't be like that. Nokia's a wonderful child," Aline responded half-heartedly.

"No, it's not. It's just a piece of electronic equipment. I wanted a granddaughter that I could love and play with." her mother lamented.

"You can do anything with Nokia that you can do with a regular child. She's really good at playing Peek-a-boo," Aline retorted bitterly. It hurt her that even her own mother couldn't warm up to her offspring.

Over time, both Aline and Fred needed to return to work full-time. They each owned and operated small businesses. Aline owned an e-cigarette shop on Monkland Avenue that she had closed for the first two months of Nokia's life, at great expense. Fred manufactured nicotine patches to help people quit smoking. He had gone into work sporadically over that period, but needed to devote more time to the business. That meant they would need to find adequate daycare for Nokia, which they feared would be difficult.

There were several Quebec-government subsidized daycare centres near their Monkland Village home. Upon investigation, however, few of them had spots available, and of those that did, most did not seem equipped to deal with Nokia's special needs. There was one, the Fingers Crossed Daycare, which sounded promising. They arranged an appointment to meet its director, Dr. Benson, who gave them a tour of the facilities.

"Nokia needs a daycare that's equipped to handle her unique requirements," Aline stressed.

"Yes, Mrs. Butterfat. Fingers Crossed is the ideal place for her," Dr. Benson assured her.

"That's good to hear. But will she be plugged in during naptime? That's critically important for her health," Aline insisted.

"Of course!" Dr. Benson declared. "All the children get plugged in during naptime, in accordance with government requirements."

"All the children?" Fred found that hard to believe.

"Yes, of course. What do you think I run here? An establishment that violates the law? We follow all Quebec daycare laws!" Dr. Benson stated emphatically.

"And what do you do to protect children like Nokia from scratches and breakage?" Aline asked nervously.

"We take that very seriously here," the director responded. "All children are wrapped in cotton when they're not in use, and their screens are cleaned each morning and afternoon. No child is allowed to touch another child's screen without supervision."

While it sounded like a most unusual daycare, it nonetheless promised to be the perfect institution for Nokia. They signed her up immediately.

Over time, however, they began to have second thoughts about Nokia's daycare. When they brought her home at the end of the day, she was frequently exhausted, as if she hadn't been charged at all during the day. When she did come home charged, she was often overexcited, with her screen blinking and evidence that she had been accessing websites that were inappropriate for her age group. Her screen was frequently smudged or scratched. Each time they called Dr. Benson to complain, he assured them that the daycare was operating to the highest standards and that they were imagining these problems.

One Friday, however, the weekly daycare newsletter confirmed their suspicions. On the front page, a large photograph with the caption "Picture of the Week: Naptime" showed twelve babies and Nokia without a single charging cable in evidence. They were being tended by two teenage workers in uniform, both swilling beer from extra-large cans. Dr. Benson stood behind them playing darts. In horror, they called the director immediately.

"Dr. Benson, you ought to be ashamed of yourself! You promised us that all the children would be plugged in during naptime," Aline began, her nasal voice sharp and accusing.

"That's right! We hold ourselves to the highest standards," came the director's reassuring voice.

"But that's an outright *lie*! Your newsletter has a photograph – the Picture of the Week – that proves the contrary!" Aline screamed into the phone.

"What? That can't be. One minute please." They heard what sounded like a hand being placed over the receiver, followed by the director's muffled voice saying, "Helen, did we publish a picture of the week in the newsletter?"

A woman's muffled voice responded, "Yes. Didn't you see it?"

"No. Show it to me," was Dr. Benson's muted reply. "Oh my!" he continued after a short pause. "Who published that picture?"

"It was your brother-in-law, Mr. Stark," said the muffled woman's voice.

"Ugh! That idiot! Fire him," the director ordered. They heard what sounded like a hand being removed from the receiver, followed by Dr. Benson's loud and clear voice over the telephone. "I've looked into the matter, Mrs. Butterfat, and I can assure you that all of the rules were followed properly. We meet – Hell, we exceed – Quebec government standards."

"But that's preposterous!" Fred jumped in. "The photo clearly shows daycare workers drinking, administrators throwing dangerous objects near the children and none of the children were being charged."

"It may appear to show that," Dr. Benson conceded, "but I assure you that the photograph is inaccurate. It's merely a trick of the light. An optical illusion."

They withdrew Nokia from the daycare immediately.

Without a viable daycare option, Aline decided to try taking Nokia to work with her. She did so with great trepidation, expecting her daughter to distract her and make it impossible to get anything done. To her surprise, however, it was a delight to have her around. To begin with, relieved from worry about how Nokia was getting on in daycare, Aline was able to focus on her business better. Customers in her e-cigarette shop enjoyed having the little one around. Aline even found that Nokia was able to help out around the shop, with an app to keep track of inventory and her camera to monitor against theft. From a developmental point of view, Nokia benefitted from social interaction with the customers and the opportunity to bond with her mother.

The experiment proved such a success that Fred was eager to take Nokia to his company, too. But Aline had grown so attached to her daughter that she refused to part with her.

After five months as new parents, the Butterfats decided it was time for them to resume going out occasionally in the evening. The first time they did so, rather than finding a babysitter they could trust, they decided to visit a movie theater with special showings for parents with young children. As they settled into their seats, an announcement over the public address system asked all parents to put their babies in airplane mode, with pacifiers in their mouths, so as not to disturb other patrons. Aline readily complied, swaddling Nokia in a blanket and plugging her cable into a nearby outlet.

As the curtain rose, they glanced around the theater at all the other babies. Unlike Nokia, who was resting peacefully, the others were fidgeting, crying, making noise, being generally disruptive. One child was flinging strained peas on the seat. Nokia would *never* do something so impertinent. During the movie, another child regurgitated on his father's sport jacket, while several others required diaper changes. With all the noise and fussing about, it was simply impossible to enjoy the film.

The experience cultivated a sense of superiority in the Butterfats. Their daughter was so much better raised, infinitely better behaved than the others.

Their esteem for their daughter grew after a gathering with new parents in their neighbourhood. The stories that other parents shared with them filled them with horror.

"Our son Jimmy still doesn't sleep through the night. We're perpetually sleep deprived. It's driving us batty," complained Horace from down the block.

"Don't get me started about teething," whined a woman with a high-pitched voice and a face that was a cross between John

Diefenbaker and the Frankenstein monster. "My daughter has been crying non-stop for the past week!"

"My Nathaniel gets a horrible diaper rash that makes him very cranky," contributed a short woman with a Liverpudlian accent. "It's impossible for us to concentrate on anything else with all the fussing."

"You've got to watch them like a hawk, too," Horace added. "Jimmy nearly rolled down the stairs once when I was distracted by the doorbell."

"And don't forget the cost of diapers," the Liverpudlian reminded them. "We spend more than the national budget of some of the smaller countries!"

Fred and Aline exchanged a knowing glance. They really had it easy. Nokia was well-behaved and gave them almost no trouble. She really was the perfect daughter.

One evening, while Fred was in the living room teaching Nokia to speak Spanish with one of her foreign language apps, the house landline rang. Aline answered it in the kitchen.

"Hello? Is this Mrs. Butterfat?" a man's voice asked.

"Speaking," Aline replied.

"This is Dr. Bertrand calling. I have great news for you!" the voice announced.

"Yes?"

"We've found your baby!" the doctor declared.

"What do you mean? We've got her right here with us," Aline uttered in bewilderment.

"No, I mean your *real* baby. You're going to laugh.... Apparently, during the delivery, I accidentally dropped my cellphone.

We mistook that for your baby. Ha ha. You'd be surprised how often something like that happens. So, what you think is your daughter is actually my cellphone." Dr. Bertrand said amiably.

A terrible fear seized Aline. "So, what are you saying?"

"Well, if you bring back my cellphone, we can give you your real daughter. Boy, this whole situation is kind of funny, you have to admit," Dr. Bertrand said with a giggle.

Aline just stared in terror at the telephone. After a long silence the doctor called out, "Mrs. Butterfat? Are you there?"

"Just a minute. Let me talk to my husband," she answered.

In tears, she dropped the receiver and ran to the living room. There she beheld the incomparably beautiful sight of father and daughter learning together in harmony, bonding together. With a lump in her throat, she explained to Fred all that Dr. Bertrand had told her. They looked at each other and then at Nokia. It did not take them long to decide how to respond. Aline returned to the phone in the kitchen.

"I'm sorry, Dr. Bertrand, but you can keep your baby," Aline began.

"But…" the doctor tried to interject, but was promptly cut off by Aline.

"We love our daughter very much. She may be different from all the other children, but we love her *because* of that. Different is good." With that, she hung up the telephone and didn't answer any subsequent calls from the hospital.

Modern Love

E lise was drowning. The weight of everyone's expectations, her own ideals, was more than she could bear, was plunging her down into the swirling waters of despair. It was hard to be a woman, a feminist, an environmentalist, a daughter, a professional, a human being with needs and desires, all at the same time. When she spoke to her parents, her friends, they all had clearly defined ideas about how she should live her life. Strangling, suffocating ideas, all with her best interest at heart. The curse of good intentions. It was difficult for her to argue against their lofty goals, their certainty, so most of the time she kept silent, turning her frustration, her alienation, her hopelessness, her rage, inward. It required a heroic effort to keep her head above the gathering waves of apathy, depression, doubt, desolation, but she was losing her will to do so.

On a cold Tuesday morning in early November, she was going through the motions of yet another empty morning rush to work: brush her teeth, toilet, shower, blow dry, skirt, blouse, stockings, flats. Soon she would stumble into the kitchen for coffee, yogurt, oatmeal, then grab her coat, run to the elevator and dash to make her bus. She was too young to settle into such a grey, drab routine. Although she had relished the challenge of her job as a branch manager for one of the big five Canadian banks, lately she found even that hollow and meaningless. What was the point of professional success? To make the bank richer? Where was the social good in that? Why couldn't being a successful career woman serve some loftier purpose?

Flicking her mahogany bang away from her eyes – it was always getting in the way – she checked her voicemail, less out of actual interest than as an act of rebellion, to alter her routine. Another message from Leonard. If nothing else, he was certainly persistent. "Hi Elise, it's me. Leonard. I've been trying to reach you. Look, it's awkward to say this on your voicemail, but I really thought we had something. You seemed spooked that it was moving so quickly. So if you want to slow things down, I'm okay with that. But please don't run away and hide. Please call me to talk about it." She sighed bitterly.

They had met at a friend's party. Her first thought was: What a boring name! Who could fall in love with a Leonard? Imagine screaming at the height of passion, 'Don't stop, *Leonard*! I love you, *Leonard*!' With a name like Leonard, he must be an accountant or an office clerk. She practically said as much to him. But he assured her it wasn't like that.

"My parents named me after Leonard Cohen," he said. "I have the soul of a poet."

"Okay," she put him on the spot, "say something poetic."

Without missing a beat, he assumed the faraway look of a stereotypical romantic poet and offered, "It's nice to meet Elise, who's more enchanting than a flock of geese."

She laughed. "Is that the best you can do?"

"Well, it was either that or 'who looks just like my niece'. That's all I got."

"Then I wouldn't quit your day job if I were you. So... what *is* your day job?" she asked.

"Oh, nothing as boring as an office clerk." He paused for effect. "I'm actually an axe murderer." For a second time she laughed. He was certainly charming.

"I didn't realize that was a lucrative profession." Elise sipped some Gewurztraminer from her glass.

"The pay's not great, but the benefits are amazing!" he deadpanned.

"I don't see your axe. Where do you keep it?" she inquired.

"Ah, in polite company a lady does not request to see a gentleman's axe," he reprimanded her in an assumed British accent.

They hit it off so well that they decided to ditch the party and spent the rest of the evening drinking cocktails at a bar atop the Manulife Centre. It turned out Leonard was a personal trainer, but he said that was just something he did to pay the bills while he finished his first novel.

"Oh, that's so exciting!" Elise exclaimed. "What are you writing about?"

Leonard reflected before answering, stealing a glance at the lights of Toronto. "The novel is about an axe murderer who meets his victims at house parties."

"No, seriously," Elise pressed.

"I really can't say," he responded earnestly. "I don't like to talk about my writing until it's finished, at least in draft form."

"Fair enough," she conceded.

"And what do *you* do, aside from chastising people with boring names? Please tell me you're not the *Toronto Star*'s poetry critic."

"How did you guess?" she responded flippantly. "But seriously, I'm a branch manager at a bank."

"That's cool," Leonard declared.

"Well, I'd *rather* say that I singlehandedly rescue orphans from starvation or clean up toxic chemical spills…."

"Not everybody can be Wonder Woman," he tried to reassure her. "Although it'd be way cool if you were…." She stuck her tongue out at him. "But really," he persisted, "having a bank manager with a conscience is important, too." He flashed a sardonic, self-deprecating smile. "In fact, the world probably needs that more than it needs yet another failed novelist."

"Don't say that! You're just getting started," she said, just to be supportive. It occurred to her that she had no idea whether he had any talent as a novelist.

"That's true, but it's an uphill struggle. I think I have unique voice and a compelling story, but everybody and his brother has a novel they're trying to flog," he responded frankly.

They talked for hours without noticing the time passing. Eventually, to their mutual surprise, the waiter cleared his throat loudly and informed them that it was 2 AM, the restaurant's closing time. At Elise's insistence they split the bill and he walked her back to her Richmond Street apartment. Elise found it the most exhilarating evening she had spent in – she couldn't remember how long. As she lay awake in bed that night replaying their impromptu date in her mind, she marvelled, *Could I have imagined that my Prince Charming would be named Leonard?*

That evening led to several other dates over a three-month period. With each meeting Elise fell deeper and deeper in love with Leonard. No-one had ever made her laugh as much as he could. She found him physically attractive, downright exciting, as well.

But, like other promising relationships she had had in the past, her ideals, her principles, got in the way. As they began to talk more seriously about the future, he mentioned the children he dreamed of having. That was a red line for Elise, who was convinced that it would be irresponsible to bring a child into the world. With the spectre of an impending global climate catastrophe, nothing could be more cynical and selfish, she thought, than to produce a child who would inevitably suffer. In fact, she judged, nothing manufactures more carbon throughout its lifetime quite like a human baby. Although she loved children and, in truth, longed to have one, she believed that the reckless behaviour of her parents' generation and those before them had foreclosed that option for her.

Without explaining herself, she withdrew from Leonard, reporting herself "unavailable" for future dates. Eventually, she stopped returning his calls, preferring to avoid him rather than addressing the issue head on. It was better that way, because if she were to explain it to him in person, she might lose her nerve and be incapable of making a clean break. Now if only he would stop calling….

She stuffed her phone into her briefcase and began her commute to work, with the icy gray waters circling around her head.

At the bank, she found herself distracted and unenthralled. She had worked like a dynamo for years to attain her position, had fixed her sights on ever higher rungs on the corporate ladder at the bank's Toronto headquarters. Yet of late she wearied of the competition, the backbiting. She did her job well. Ran a tight ship. But the men who worked underneath her resented her, called her a bitch – and worse – behind her back. That type of bigotry used to fuel her determination to succeed, just to teach them. But lately, it just discouraged her, deepened her hopelessness.

Is this what I really wanted from my life, she wondered, as she prepared the tellers for opening, verifying that they had sufficient cash for the day. *Isn't it ironic that the girl who took part in every protest in college spends her days making Bay Street richer?* Today she would await the corporate headquarters' new prime rate, in response to yesterday's Bank of Canada adjustment. That would have implications for all the bank's accounts and loan products. She would also continue training the new mortgage officer, who had started on Monday. None of it filled her with any enthusiasm.

During her lunch break, she took a walk to clear her head. Instinctively, her feet carried her to the nearby University of Toronto St. George campus, where her life had held so much promise as a student. What had gone wrong? She was successful professionally, had a good network of friends. Yet it all seemed so pointless. It surprised her that her disaffection had even displaced her nostalgia for her *alma mater*, which had brought her such joy in the past. Her melancholy eyes were drawn to a billboard ad for children's clothing depicting four well-dressed toddlers. Why was the world so messed up? Why did a greedy, lazy civilization have to mess up a perfectly good planet for those children?

Wiping away a stray tear, she returned to the bank and spent most of the afternoon in videoconferences with corporate head-quarters. When she emerged near the end of the day, it was time for the closing rituals: supervising the reconciliation of accounts, tallying the tellers' cash rolls, bundling and forwarding cheques for processing, securing the tills. It was all so routine and mean-ingless. *If this is all my life is going to be,* she reflected, *it's simply not worth it.*

After surviving work, Elise met her friends for dinner and drinks at a Polynesian Bar in Parkdale. She had been close with Charli since high school. Maude, a dentist who worked in the same building as Charli did, had joined their circle of friends in recent years. Charli had chosen the venue and it was exactly her kind of place: kitschy, garishly appointed and raucous fun. At other times, Elise might have allowed herself to loosen up and get into the swing of things. But in her present humour, with the world closing in around her, she found the artificial grass-covered bar, the waiters in loud Hawaiian shirts, the Polynesian music, off-putting. She sat rigidly, nursing her Cobra's Fang cocktail, a plastic smile fixed on her drawn face.

Charli, her jet-black hair cropped short, peered through her round, crimson glasses into Elise's bloodshot eyes and said with concern, "You don't look good at all, girl, even in this light. And with you, that's saying something. Is it that Leonard thing?"

Elise nodded sadly. "I really liked him. Why can't I find someone I like that also shares my values?"

"I know it's cliché, darling, but men are pigs," Charli said, as she fiddled with the frilly orange umbrella on her Mai Tai.

Maude vehemently agreed. "Amen to that!" she said, as she took an ample swig of her Jungle Bird and leaned back against the oval back of her rattan wood chair. Her shoulder-length hair was a bit too blond to be natural and she wore too much makeup, making her otherwise attractive features appear somewhat grotesque. "Men only want you on their own terms. They're happy with you when you're not too successful, when you don't outshine them, when you cater to their needs. But if you assert what *you* want, they'll steer clear of you and call you a ballbuster."

"That's not fair. Leonard wasn't a bad guy..." Elise began.

"Even the good ones are pigs," Maude interrupted.

"*Especially* the good ones. They're the *worst*," Charli snapped.

"Absolutely!" Maude agreed. "They're all kind and sweet and understanding – 'Oh, whatever you *wish, dear*!' 'I really want *your* opinion.' But then they turn all Mussolini on you and start dictating what you can and can't do. 'I don't like you spending so much time with your friends!' 'Don't wear *that*! It makes you look fat.' 'You can't take that job! It would mean too many weekends and night shifts.' Then, when you've twisted your life into a pretzel to accommodate them, you come home early from work to find them in your bed with their physiotherapist."

Elise winced. Maude had recently divorced her husband because of his serial infidelity. It was hard for Elise to talk about her own misery when Maude always brought everything back to herself. This is what always happened, she reflected. They never listened – truly *listened* – to what she said. They ran circles around her with their clever banter and their high ideals, but they never heard how broken she was inside, how perilously close she was to the precipice. Didn't they care?

There was a commotion in the bar, as the bartender called out "Volcano Bowl" in a cryptic voice over the din of eerie island music.

Watching the waiter bring a large, smoking bowl to impressed guests at the next table, Charli purred, feeling the effects of the alcohol, "That's where I'm in better shape than either of you. I don't need men for *anything*."

Elise forced an awkward smile, but inwardly she was disturbed. *They don't* want *to understand,* she thought morosely to herself. *I don't hate men. My father's a man and he wants nothing more than my happiness. My brothers are men and, even though we view the world very differently, I love them dearly. I love men in general. I'm hoping for a long-term relationship with a man one day. And I really liked Leonard....*

She brushed her dark bang out of her coffee bean eyes and made a half-hearted effort to set her friends straight. "Well, Charli, I kinda *like* men."

"I've *always* thought that was a shame, dear. But chaqu'un ses gouts..." Charli retorted, a lascivious gleam in her eye. She signalled the waiter to bring her another cocktail.

Maude laughed. "Oh, Charli, you're incorrigible!"

The alcohol worked differently on each of them. It endowed Charli with an exaggerated bravado that concealed her vulnerability, made her seem callous and uncaring. Maude became louder and more animated, less boring and inhibited than she felt she was otherwise. But Elise was a sad drunk. She just became more morose and bitter.

"Listen, Elise, you had no choice," Maude said as a blast of cold air burst in from the street when another patron opened the front door, creating a surreal impression in the Hawaiian surroundings. "You can't compromise everything you hold dear just because some man wants you to. You're a good person and a committed environmentalist. You think about bigger things than 'me, me, me'. If he's more concerned about reproducing himself than he is about social responsibility, you're better off without him," Maude said, before tucking into the garlic knots the waiter brought for the table.

"Yeah. You've got your career. You're an independent woman. You don't need someone who doesn't fit into your value system," Charli added.

"I suppose…" Elise muttered half-heartedly.

Why do I do this? I've hung around with them for years, yet I don't think I see the world like they do. And, though I pride myself on being a strong, confident woman, I never feel capable of arguing with them.

Instead of restoring her, allowing her to open the valve to release pent-up steam, the night out with friends just intensified her despair. *I'm alone*, she thought. *No-one hears me. I suffer alone.* She felt her head plunge below the surface, black clouds above choking out the faint remains of her once dazzling sun.

She fared no better at her parents' home the following evening. Elise always felt out of place in her parents overheated, over-lit Mcmansion. The whole house reeked of excess. Her parents had always acted irresponsibly, sneered at her efforts to conserve, to recycle, to compost, to avoid meat. Of course she loved them, but love and anger, love and contempt, were by no means mutually exclusive. Lately, visiting her parents had become an unpleasant, tension-laden filial chore for Elise.

Over dinner, they said little, focusing on the fettucini alfredo as a refuge from conflict. After dinner, however, her parents ambushed her, as they often did.

"So what happened to that guy you were seeing?" her mother asked. "Leonard."

Elise had dreaded that question. "It didn't work out," she muttered, dropping her dark eyes to the floor to avert her mother's probing gaze.

"Why ever not? You two seemed *perfect* for each other." Elise's father implored his wife with a stern glance to exercise restraint, but she made a show of ignoring him.

"It's not so simple, Mom."

"Isn't it? If you like someone, get along with him, that's the basis of a good relationship," her mother reasoned.

Elise testily brushed her errant bang away from her eyes. "Listen, we just had different worldviews. Different goals in life."

"You're *thirty-two* years old, dear! You can't keep searching for perfection. Leonard's a decent guy and you worked well together. Why do you need more than that?" Her mother's husky voice rose as she said this.

"Life is hard enough without complicating it unnecessarily with misplaced principles," her father said. "Don't make it harder on yourself."

"Make up your mind, Dad," she retorted flippantly. "You always tell me that life is beautiful. Now you say it's hard. Which is it?" Her father's so-called wisdom always got under her skin.

"The truth is that it's both," he replied, ignoring her sarcasm. "So much in life is beautiful. Nature. Art. Love. But that's only part of the story. There's also drudgery. Failure. Sickness. Death. You've got to embrace the beauty whenever you can, because there's hardship lurking around the corner."

His words struck a chord. Of late, she had had more than her share of drudgery, of misery. But whose fault was it that she couldn't embrace the beauty? *Their* irresponsible choices and the actions of countless others *like them* foreclosed her chance at happiness. *How can he lecture me on life, pretending to be the sage, the great philosopher,* she simmered, *when he messed everything up for me? And why am I incapable of saying that to him? I'm no longer a seven-year-old girl. Why do they make me feel like I am?*

"By the same token," her father continued in his slow, professorial manner, oblivious to her contempt, "life is both too short and too long. The prime of life passes by in the wink of an eye. You can't afford to waste it. But life's far too long to spend it all alone, Elly."

It was her mother's turn to tug at her heartstrings. "And, if you want children, you have to move quickly." She sighed. "Oh, how your father and I would *love* to have grandchildren…"

Elise remembered learning in Bible school how Pharaoh had hardened his heart at the end of each of Moses' plagues. That was exactly the effect of her mother's entreaty on her. Her entire countenance changed, assumed a hard and nasty aspect. For the balance of the evening, she let her parents talk, largely without responding, save the occasional nod or hollow reply to a question, her eyes glazed, her heart impervious. When she could endure it no more, she stared icily at her mother and declared peremptorily,

"I've got to go." Without warmth, she ritually kissed her parents on their cheeks, fetched her coat and went, leaving her parents puzzled and concerned.

That night Elise was unable to sleep. Her parents infuriated her, as always. And, yet again, she had failed to stand up for herself. As usual, she rehashed the conversation in her head, inserting what she ought to have said, instead of her weak replies. Why couldn't she respond like that when they were in front of her? Why did they still have such power over her?

When she finally drifted off, she was troubled by disturbing dreams and images that caused her to lurch violently in bed. In one dream, she was at her office at the bank when she heard plaintive screaming. Searching for the source of the cries, she found her mother and Charli in matching scarlet bathrobes playing cards at the tellers' counters. She asked in annoyance why nobody was feeding the baby. "What baby?" Charli asked and continued placing cards face up on the counter. To Elise's mystification, they were all the King of Hearts. "The one that's screaming," she snapped uneasily, but they didn't pay any attention to her. Fear welling up in the pit of her stomach, Elise crept up to a large black carriage near the bank entrance. With great trepidation, outright terror, she lifted a black lace veil and peered inside, but there was nothing there, except for the shards of a shattered mirror. She woke up in a cold sweat, breathing heavily.

All the ensuing weekend, Elise remained in her apartment, in bed most of the time. She ate little and didn't shower or change out of her pajamas. Her frustration and despair were complete. She had submerged completely beneath the dark gray waters, which had snuffed out all light, all hope from above. She was on the cusp of a momentous decision, something she had contemplated for weeks. All that remained was to convince herself, to overcome her innate hesitation, the doubts that always paralyzed her.

I've never really fit in anywhere, she reasoned, scratching at her curved ebony eyebrow. *Not at home, not with my friends, not at work. Sure, there was U. of T., but that was different, an artificial world before the trauma of real life begins. And, I hate to admit it, but Dad's right. If I'm miserable now, when I'm young and healthy and, well, pretty, what hope do I have in the future. I'm destined to live alone to fight other people's battles. To clean up other people's messes. I can't do that. I just can't…. There's really only one way out, but could I?* She hesitated momentarily at the brink, but then coldly made her decision. *In the end, it didn't matter,* she told herself. *My soul is already dead.*

Sitting on the bed in her studio apartment, the stale aroma of last night's almost untouched take-out Udon noodles heavy in the air, she finally worked up the courage to do what she knew she would inevitably do since the waters started gathering around her. She couldn't carry on any longer. She had thought about it many times. Planned it out. She wouldn't slit her wrists or hang herself. Wouldn't jump out a window. That would require a quick decisive act that she did not have in her. She would lose her nerve. Instead, she would swallow pills, one-by-one. Slow. Steady. Incremental.

She considered writing a goodbye note. Wasn't that what's traditionally done in these situations? She fetched a pen and a pad from a drawer in the kitchen and returned to bed, staring vacantly at the pad. She had no clue where to begin. What could she say that wouldn't make it worse? Eventually, not even bothering to push her hair away from her eyes, she wrote a terse sentence, "It's better this way," and pushed the pad aside.

She opened a bottle of extra strength Acetaminophen that she fished out of the medicine cabinet in the bathroom and brought it to the kitchen counter with a large cocktail glass of water. Predictably, it had expired, but that didn't matter for her purpose. She took a long last look around her apartment. This was all her life had amounted to: a few paintings, a faux leather sofa, some photographs of her friends and family. Her phone started ringing, but she ignored it. What could it matter now anyway? Better to do it quickly and not prolong the misery. She placed thirty tablets on the counter – *that should be enough to do the job.*

She began ingesting them one-by-one, with the help of the water.

One. Two. Three. Four....

How would they manage at the bank, she wondered. Oh well, I'm not indispensable. There are plenty of people waiting to replace me.

Five. Six. Seven....

What would Charli and Maud say? Won't they have a lot of clever, knowing comments to make the next time they get together.

Eight. Nine. Ten. Eleven....

So far, it wasn't so bad. She wondered how long it would take.

Twelve. Thirteen. Fourteen. Fifteen....

She ran out of water and needed to refill the glass at the kitchen sink. How surreal it seemed!

Sixteen. Seventeen. Eighteen....

It was getting more difficult now, like her body didn't want any more.

Nineteen. Twenty....

What would her parents say? Maybe now they would understand what they had done to her all these years.

Twenty-one. Twenty-two....

She feared that she might vomit if she swallowed any more, but she had to continue.

Twenty-three. Twenty-four....

But on second thought, she really didn't want her parents to suffer. They would take it very hard.... This wasn't about them, though. It was for her.

Twenty-five. Twenty-six....

Yes, it was best not to think of the others. She was the only one that mattered. But why did it have to be so hard to swallow?

Twenty-seven.

It took a herculean effort for her to ingest the last few pills, but she persevered.

Twenty-eight.... Twenty-nine....

Only one more, then it would be over. Come on.... Come on....

Thirty.

Once the deed was done, it was only a matter of waiting for the peace that would come to her at last. She ambled back to bed and decided to see who had called. Her last phone call. Oh, it was Leonard again. Absently, she played his message. "Hi Elise! It's Leonard. Leonard Cohen. Remember me? I thought I'd try one last time. I'm not much of a singer – maybe even less than a poet – but I thought maybe if I gave it a shot...." He then launched into a campy, cringeworthy rendition of *Hey, That's No Way to Say Goodbye*, complete with glib word substitutions and double *entendres*. When he finished, his voice turned earnest and he begged, "Please call me, Elise. I think we have something to build on. Don't throw away the best thing in our lives."

For a brief instant, the waters above her head parted, giving her a glimpse of a light long extinguished. Suddenly, she was seized with a fierce longing to see him, to hold him. But what had she done? It was already too late. She quickly grabbed the phone and frantically punched in 911. Her next call was to her father, who answered on the fourth ring. Before he could say 'hello,' she pounced on him. "Daddy, please come here *now*!!!"

He could hear the desperation in her voice. "What's wrong, princess?"

"I need you, Daddy! I want to *live*! I want to live...."

Memory

"What's wrong? You can't seem to settle down," my wife asked, a little annoyed that I wasn't allowing her to sleep either.

"Sorry. It's just that I remembered something. About Mom and Dad," I replied.

She propped herself up on her pillow and turned to face me in the dark, her body silhouetted by the ambient light that escaped through the folds of the curtains. "What is it?" she asked with the concern, the solicitude, the guilt of the spouse with two living parents.

"It's just…. Just something that happened when I was young, that I'd forgotten about." It was hard for me to explain.

"What happened?"

"I don't really know. That's what's bugging me," I recounted. "One year, when I was about ten or twelve years old, we spent a summer vacation in Lake Placid. At one point on that trip, I remember sitting in the car with my sisters at a strip mall, listening to the radio. We were waiting for my parents while they went into an office of some sort, next to a Price Chopper supermarket. When they came out, they were both crying."

"Why?" Despite the late hour, the early morning meeting with her producer scheduled for 8:00 AM, my wife's curiosity was piqued.

"That's just it. I have no idea. It's one of those childhood memories that gets forgotten. Gets buried under decades of life. Maybe I repressed it. But for whatever reason, it came to me quite vividly now."

"Hmmm…" she considered, "Maybe Ingrid'll know. Why don't you ask her when we see her on Friday?"

"Good idea, Mandy," I concurred, as I started to knead her back with my palms to help her succumb to sleep.

That Friday night, my wife, my three boys and I ascended the steps to Ingrid's Outremont townhouse, as we have done for most of the past decade. Ingrid is my sister, the middle child, two years older than I, four years junior to Emma. Intelligent, good-natured, fun-loving, she was always a delight to be around. When I was born, she made it her mission to look out for me, to be my guardian angel. We were inseparable as children and have remained so as adults with families of our own. We live a short drive from each other, she in Outremont, me in an upper duplex in the Plateau. And we bring our families together for dinner every Friday night in her dining room. She would never allow my wife and me to host. It was her prerogative as big sister. At times I found that hard to swallow, even downright insulting. We're both in our forties with only twenty-two months between us. I own my own small business, am an independent person in my own right. Why should the tyranny of birth order keep me perpetually the supplicant? Yet that's just her way, and it's hard to hold a grudge against Ingrid. Over time I grew to accept it. Even after her divorce and her Leukemia diagnosis, she continued to preside over dinner as affably as ever, happy to remain in command, to enjoy her pride of place.

On this particular Friday, Ingrid was weaker than normal, still feeling the effects of the immunotherapy treatment she had received earlier in the week. As a concession, she had allowed Mandy and me to prepare the food. Her spirits were as high as ever, though, and she clearly delighted in having her baby brother in her home.

After dinner, the children descended to the basement to play Ping-Pong and billiards, while the adults retired to the living room with digestifs. I installed myself on a brown leather armchair, sipping a glass of *Sortilège* maple whiskey liqueur, and waited for my sister to finish her savage critique of the "unprincipled principal" at her son's school to question her about our parents.

"So there he goes again. He makes a rule, but it doesn't apply to his own daughter. When I catch him with his hands in the cookie jar," she mimed a ridiculous parody of the principal's shocked face to play to her audience, "he responds with more evasions, half-truths and lies. Now *that's* integrity," Ingrid concluded.

"Wow! What a pig!" Mandy chipped in sympathetically, shaking her telegenic head from side to side to dislodge an errant blonde lock from her eyes.

"No, I wouldn't go that far…" Ingrid paused for comedic effect, then continued, "Okay, I would. He *is* a pig! OINK!" Her deep, sonorous laugh was infectious, even if her voice was hoarser, rawer than usual.

I waited for the laughter to die down before jumping in, "Ing, do you remember when we were kids we spent a couple of weeks in Lake Placid one summer?"

"Of course! We actually went there a couple of times, but *you* might have been too young to remember the first time, Squirt." Her response was encouraging. I was confident she would help me get to the bottom of this.

"Well, I was thinking of a time when I was about ten or so. Mom and Dad went into some sort of office next to a supermarket in a strip mall and came out crying...." I let my voice trail off, waiting for Ingrid to indicate her recognition and supply details.

"Are you sure I was there? I don't remember that," she pronounced after a brief pause, ruffling her short, boyish hair with her lavender-painted nails.

"Yes, the three of us waited in the car, eating Carvel ice cream. The Rolling Stones' *Sympathy for the Devil* was playing over the radio and you and Emma were singing 'Hoo, hoo!' into your fists, pretending they were microphones. I remember dropping my scoop off the cone and messing up Mom's station wagon. You burst out laughing, while Emma told me I was going to get into big trouble when Mom came back. Doesn't ring any bells?" I queried.

She wrinkled her brow while she plumbed the depths of her memory. With every passing second, I grew convinced that I would get no help from Ingrid, after all. Suddenly, her face brightened, bringing to mind the luminous, feminine, irrepressible Ingrid of old, and she blurted out, "No! You're all mixed up! That didn't happen in Mom's car. That was in Dad's new Chrysler sedan. That's why Emma and I tried to clean it up frantically. He was so proud of that car and wasn't thrilled about us eating in it in the first place. Also, I'm pretty sure it was Baskin and Robbins ice cream, because I had their Jamoca Almond Fudge, which Carvel doesn't sell.... And I don't remember Mom and Dad crying."

Her recollection surprised me. I was pretty sure I had dirtied my mother's station wagon. In my mind's eye, I can still see myself sprawling out in the cargo hold, which we kids had christened the 'back-back.' I was leaning over toward the back seat, where my sisters were sitting. Gravity did the rest, making a gooey mess on the upholstery behind the driver's seat.

"Also," Ingrid continued her critique, "that wasn't in *Lake Placid*. That was when we stayed in Alexandria Bay."

"I'm positive it *was* Lake Placid. We started out at the Marcy Hotel. Do you remember the Marcy?" I turned to Mandy to explain, "Mom said it was a fancy hotel that she used to stay at when she was a kid. But by then it was really run down, so we moved out into an efficiency just outside of town." I pivoted back to Ingrid. "But I was really wondering why they were *crying....*"

"Sorry, Squirt!" Ingrid cut in. "The Marcy was in *Alexandria Bay*! It was a horrible place! We couldn't sleep all night because there was a mouse squeaking underneath the bed all night."

"Sounds like quite the place!" Mandy chipped in.

"It was *awful*," I agreed. "That'd be a fun topic for a local interest spot, don't you think? Luxury hotels that've gone to pot? But I don't remember a mouse. There was a giant spider on the wall that freaked us all out, and it was a cricket that kept us up all night, not a mouse. I shared a bed with Dad, while Ingrid and Emma huddled together with Mom. I don't think any of us slept that night. It was definitely in Lake Placid, though."

"No, it *wasn't!*" Ingrid persisted, with lively defiance in her warm bronze eyes. "Squirt, you wouldn't remember your own name properly if it weren't printed on your driver's license!"

My eldest niece, a spitting image of her father, who had been listening at the door found our bickering amusing. "Are you sure you two grew up in the same family? You can't agree on anything!" she chortled.

She had a point. How could we remember these events so differently?

"You know, now that I think about it, I believe I *do* remember them going into a real estate office when we were in Alexandria Bay," Ingrid piped in. "I think they used to own property in New York State when we were young. Maybe it had something to do with that."

"But why were they crying when they came out?" I persisted.

"You know, I don't believe they were," replied Ingrid thoughtfully. "Now that you mention it, I think they were *laughing* when they returned to the car. I don't think even the ice cream you smeared on Dad's upholstery spoiled the mood."

"Laughing?" I asked incredulously. "That's not at all what I remember. Why would they have been laughing?"

"Oh, come on! Dad's sense of humour? It always came out in spades during a vacation. And, now that we have our own kids, I'm convinced that Mom and Dad liked to steal away from us at times to have their own private moments. To share their own private jokes." Though drawn and pallid, Ingrid's face when she said this was the picture of tranquility, almost rapture.

"Dad certainly *did* have an odd sense of humour," I recalled with a laugh. "You remember his awful trapezoid joke?"

Ingrid groaned. "He never tired of it. It was so *bad*, yet he kept telling it to people."

"Tell it to me!" my niece begged.

"Well, okay," I consented. "What did the general say when he fell into a misshapen rectangle that his enemy placed in his path to ensnare him?"

"I give up," my niece said.

Ingrid supplied the punchline with mock drama, "Oh no! It's a *trapezoid*!!"

My niece guffawed, then went downstairs to share it with the other children.

"You know, I heard that Cheap Trick song the other day," Ingrid volunteered. "'Bout Mommy and Daddy being weird? It made me smile because it's like it was written for them."

"I miss them," I said reflectively.

"Well," Ingrid sighed wistfully, "I may see them soon...."

"Don't talk like that, Ing!" Mandy commanded. "The treatment's going well. You're going to be *fine*."

"I hope you're right...." she replied without conviction, grasping the rolled arm of the chesterfield she was installed upon for support.

The conversation shifted to provincial politics, as it often did, but we soon noticed that Ingrid was too fatigued to keep the party going. So Mandy and I helped her clean up from dinner, before returning home. As usual, we had had a wonderful evening, but we felt the storm clouds gathering ominously in the distance.

As I lay down to sleep that night, I remained troubled about the episode in the parking lot all those years ago. I found Ingrid's version of the event unsatisfying. So many details of her account were at odds with my own recollection. Surely, I couldn't have been that far off the mark, could I?

On Sunday morning I decided to call Emma to see if she could shed any light on my mystery. Emma had moved to England after she graduated McGill and had little contact with the family thereafter. I had hoped that our mother's extended illness, our parents' passing might bring us closer together, but the truth was that we were very different people, had incompatible outlooks on life.

The five-hour time difference meant that it was early afternoon in London. I waited on the line listening to the international ringtone, two short bursts alternating with a short silence, until I heard her voice, her accent altered by many years overseas, on the line.

"Hi Emma," I began cheerfully, "How's life on your side of the pond?"

"Oh, it's you, Thomas." She sounded disappointed. "I'm rather busy actually."

"I see. If you'd prefer, I could call you later in the week," I volunteered.

She hesitated for a moment, thinking over my proposition, then decided, "No… No… I suppose we can talk now." Why did she always make me feel like I was an imposition? It had been that way ever since she entered CEGEP, Québec's two-year bridge between high school and university. She was always too cool, too important, to waste her time with her baby brother. It wasn't that way when we were kids.

"How's Quentin?" I inquired politely.

"Fine… Fine…" she had the annoying habit of repeating answers twice, distractedly, as if to underscore the effort she required to hold a conversation with me. "And how's *your* wife? Amanda?"

"She's well, thanks. The boys are well, too. We had a great time with Ing and the kids on Friday. Too bad you weren't there," I responded jovially, ignoring the slight.

There was an awkward silence. Was she reading her texts while talking to me?

"Listen, Emma," I jumped straight to the point, "I was hoping you could help me out with something."

"Huh? What would you need *my* help with? You know I'm not going to be back in Canada for a while." She was already trying to wriggle out of any possible obligations.

"No. It's nothing like that," I assured her. It was so frustrating to talk to her sometimes. "I'm just trying to remember something that happened when we were kids. I thought that you might be able to shed some light on it."

"Alright," she conceded, "shoot."

I briefly explained my quest and the discrepancies between Ingrid's and my accounts. Over the phone, it was impossible to see if my tale brought a flash of recognition to her eyes.

"What could that possibly matter? That was almost forty years ago!!!"

"I know," I admitted, "but it's been bothering me. I really need to know. Does this ring a bell for you?"

"I guess it *would* matter to you. You were always their favourite," she said, with venom.

"Maybe Mom's," I conceded with annoyance. "For reasons I could never understand, Dad always favoured you. You never had a kind word for him, always rode him for his accent, his smoking, for everything. Yet you were always his special girl. Poor Ingrid always tried so hard, yet she always played second fiddle to you."

"Oh, you and Ingrid always saw only what you wanted to. Our parents were the most *selfish* people I have ever met. We were just *impositions* for them." I could picture her nose wrinkling, her jaw clenching, as she said this.

"Look, I didn't call to fight with you. If you don't know any-thing about it, let's just forget it." I had promised myself that I wouldn't let her draw me into an unpleasant confrontation, as she always did. Clearly, I had failed.

"Well," she hesitated, "I think I do remember the vacation you're talking about."

"And?" I asked testily.

"Well, I think you've both jumbled different vacations together. To begin with, while *you're* right, the Marcy was in Lake Placid, the summer I believe you are referring to was the year cousin William got married in Saratoga Springs and we stayed in a cottage near Lake George. When we arrived, we had to pick up the keys from a real estate office nearby, which was in a plaza with a Safeway supermarket and a Baskin Robbins. While they were getting the keys, you and Ingrid went to get ice cream from Baskin and Robbins, while I got milk and other staples for the cottage from Safeway. Mystery solved."

"Well, not quite...." I ruminated. "I'm sure it was a Price Chopper, rather than a Safeway...."

"No, it was definitely a Safeway!" she protested.

"I suppose that's not really important. But why were they crying when they returned to the car?"

"They weren't. They were *yelling* at each other." She spoke as if she were scolding an ignorant child.

"Well, why would they have been yelling?" I asked with skepticism.

"Because they always *did*. They fought *all the time*! Don't you remember? That's why I stopped going on vacation with you all once I was old enough to stay by myself. I couldn't *take* all their bickering. They were always at one another's throats."

"Oh, come on! Of course they argued. But no more than most people. Probably a lot less." My boys would probably also say that Mandy and I fought a lot, I reasoned, but that wasn't really true. Ours was a loving relationship, a playful one, just not in front of the boys. From the unguarded moments I caught – the glimpses, the tender glances when they thought I wasn't looking – and from the effect Dad's death had on mom, I know the same was true of my parents.

"I sometimes wonder whether you're wilfully blind, Thomas! You see everything through romantic lenses," she chided. "At any rate, Dad was in a foul mood because of the drive, perhaps he was hungry, too, and the two of them were at each other's throats. I'm sure it didn't help that they came back to find that you had spilled ice cream all over the loaner car that they were driving."

"Loaner? Weren't we in Mom's car?" I asked.

"No! I think Mom had an accident in her car and it was being repaired. We drove a loaner down to the States that year," Emma recalled.

"I guess I forgot that, but I remember the rushed clean-up job you and Ing did, using a Mad magazine and water because we didn't have any Kleenex or paper towels." The image made me smile.

"That's right. The more we rubbed, the more we embedded the ice cream into the fabric of the seat! And oh, did it smell!" Emma's voice became more animated.

"When was the last time we all laughed together like that? I miss it," I declared nostalgically, believing I might actually have been reaching her for the first time in many years.

"Oh, *grow up*, will you Thomas?" she countered acidly. I couldn't fathom – still can't fathom – the depths of resentment in her heart. I wanted to tell her to give up her bitterness. That, now that they were dead, it was time to find a way to forgive them – forgive us all – for whatever it was that had poisoned her so. But I realized it would be pointless. So I said nothing, leaving a dead silence on the line.

"Anyway, I've got to go," she announced peremptorily. "It's been good to hear from you."

"Emma?" I called out suddenly before she could hang up. It occurred to me that she might not know about Ingrid's illness. I desperately wanted to tell her, to prompt her to set things right before it was too late, but I didn't know if Ingrid would approve and I couldn't betray my dearest Ingrid. So I held my tongue, a lump forming in my throat.

"Yes?"

"Let's talk again soon," I muttered, upset with myself for letting the moment pass. Life is a chronicle of wasted opportunities.

"Goodbye, Thomas," was all she said before disconnecting.

I felt hollow, hopeless after my conversation with Emma. And I was still no closer to discovering what had happened that day. Each of us had very different recollections. Which of us was right? Were we all mixed up? I decided to explore a little further.

From what I could discern on the internet, the Marcy Hotel was indeed in Lake Placid, not Alexandria Bay. And there are no Safeway supermarkets in New York State, nor have there ever been. On the other hand, there are Price Choppers in Lake Placid, Alexandria Bay and Lake George.

I also scoured through old family photo albums. My mother had been an avid photographer and the unofficial curator of our family history. She left behind eight thick ivory-coloured photo albums chronicling all our major events, milestones, holidays and family vacations. When she passed, Ingrid and I each claimed four albums; Emma had not wanted any. The three summer vacations were all documented in a single album that remained in my possession, annotated with dates and labels in my mother's efficient script. As I scanned those faded three-by-five snapshots of a bygone era, I beheld my parents in their strength and vigour, Emma before her estrangement, the five of us swimming, laughing, smiling as a unit, with common purpose. A loving family. Whole.

Yet the photos shed little light on my quest, save the chronology of our vacations and the reason we all recalled different cars. During the summer in Alexandria Bay, both my father's grey sedan and my mother's cherry red station wagon made their appearance in the photos. No doubt my mother must have driven us first, to be joined a day or two later by my father when he could get away from work. A year later, in Lake Placid, we appeared to be driving a baby blue sedan that I did not recognize. Perhaps that was the loaner that Emma had referred to. The following year, when we travelled to Lake George, only my father's sedan was in evidence. There was nothing to indicate during which of the summers the incident took place, what my parents had been doing at the office or what it all meant.

So each of us had misremembered key elements of the story. Were our recollections the products of our own personalities, the lenses we brought with us, our lives ever since? Did they stem from the different stories we told ourselves afterwards? Had we all remembered only fragments of the truth and then reconstructed our memories to tell a coherent story? In any event, we were all unreliable witnesses.

I found this terribly troubling. Did this mean the past was unknowable? Are all our memories simply fabrications or reconstructions, like books and movies 'based on true events'? Now that my parents were dead, was there nothing I could hold on to that was true and certain?

I guess I'll never know what happened on that trip. In some ways, I feel farther from the truth than when I started. I can't even say why it matters so much to me. What was I hoping to find anyway? Some kind of fight? An affair? A miscarriage? Would learning anything of that nature truly make me happier? Perhaps they're entitled to their secrets even in the grave.

The idyllic youth I believe I had is gone. My parents are gone. Emma, too, has departed, although by her own choice. These will never return. All that remains, aside from faded photographs and broken memories, is my beloved Ingrid – my anchor, my protector, my Polaris. I suppose all I can do is treasure her while I can, before her flame, too, is forever extinguished from my firmament.

Chat Room

Painmaker: Any1 on?

Painmaker increased IG-100 MagnaGuard's gear to level XI

DragonPrincess: Hiya Pain!

Painmaker: Hi.

DragonPrincess: Haven't seen u for a while.

Painmaker: Glad ur on. I needed to talk to some1.

Painmaker: Been dealing with ****. Life's been rough.

MINI CheeseJedi just promoted Jolee Bindo to 7-star

DragonPrincess: What's been going on, Pain?

DragonPrincess: Congrats Cheese!

Painmaker: idk... My whole life has fallen apart, Princess.

MINI CheeseJedi: ty

DragonPrincess: OMG! That sounds awful, Pain. What happened?

Painmaker: Well, I've never had many friends.

Painmaker: I'm pretty much a computer geek. Kinda awkward socially.

SuicideMuffin (Guild leader): We're all your friends, Painmaker!

Painmaker: High school's been touch.

Painmaker: **** typo! Tough, not touch. Used to get bullied in middle school. Now it's not like that anymore, but people pretty much ignore me.

Painmaker: Thanks Suicide!

Painmaker: But last year, this guy came to my school from another city. He was also a computer nerd & somewhat of a misfit. We hit it off immediately

Painmaker: & became great friends. He's always at my house or I'm at his. We like the same things. Computers. This game. The same classic rock music.

DragonPrincess: That's great!

Painmaker: U can't imagine how great that felt – to have a friend at long last. After all those years of being isolated. Either picked on or invisible.

Squonk: Hey, any1 know a good counter for bad batch?

Painmaker: After we got to know each other well, he started to open up to me about his past. He told me his deep dark secret.

MINI CheeseJedi: Ooooh! Getting interesting!

DragonPrincess: So, can u tell us? We don't know who he is.

Painmaker: Before he moved here, he got in trouble with the law & even went to juvenile detention.

DragonPrincess: Wow!

SuicideMuffin (Guild leader): Use ur rebels, CLS lead. Kill Echo first.

Painmaker: Yeah. His parents were getting divorced & it got nasty. He couldn't handle it & went off the rails. He hit the bottle, drugs, u name it. Stole from neighbourhood shops.

Darth_Poutine: Or JMLS if u have him. Cuts thru bad batch like butter :)

Painmaker: Got caught several times – says he thinks he wanted to get caught to punish his folks – & after several warnings, the judge threw him in juvy.

DragonPrincess: That sounds rough.

KenobiCanuck increased General Grievous's gear to level XII

KenobiCanuck applied a Zeta upgrade to Force Leap (Commander Ahsoka Tano)

KenobiCanuck: That's what I'm talking about!!!

Painmaker: After a while, with lots of counseling help, he got back on track & his mom moved to my city to give him a fresh start at a new school, where no1 knew of his problems.

DragonPrincess: Congrats Canuck!

Squonk: I wish I had him Poutine!

Painmaker: He told me because I'd become his 1st close friend in years & he trusted me. But he swore me to secrecy.

MINI CheeseJedi: Nice, KenobiCanuck!

Painmaker: Everything was going just fine – the best it's been in years – but then this year someone else joined our class from another school. A grill

Painmaker: **** autocorrect!!! A girl.

Painmaker: She's really pretty. I really like her. But I was too shy to say anything to her.

DragonPrincess: That's so exciting!! What's she like?

Painmaker: I'm no poet, but she's like the freshness of a fall day.

DragonPrincess: That's so sweet!

Painmaker: She makes me think of that Genesis song from Three Sides Live. Do u know Evidence of Autumn? She's like an angel who fills everything with light.

Squonk: Any rebel squad, Suicide? Or do I need Chewy3PO? Don't have him yet.

DragonPrincess: Hey, u're a bit young to be a Genesis fan, aren't u?

Painmaker: Why? I got into them & other old groups on Spotify. It's better than the **** that counts as music today!

Painmaker: How old are u, Princess?

DragonPrincess: Uh, let's just say I'm a bit older....

Painmaker: Oh. Anyway, I try to sit near her in class whenever I can, but she never seems to notice.

SuicideMuffin (Guild leader): U want to use Han to stun Echo first or it'll get nasty. Don't need Chewy3PO.

Painmaker: She was all I could think about. I kept trying to go to events & clubs that she might go to just to see her.

Painmaker: Once, I was so nervous near her that I tripped over someone's knapsack & fell into her. I was so embarrassed. But I smelled her hair. Such a pretty smell. Like an apple orc

Squonk: Thx.

Painmaker: Orchard. I can't get that wonderful smell out of my mind.

Territory War Preview Phase has begun.

DragonPrincess: So get the courage to talk to her Pain!

Painmaker: Wait! I'm not finished.

Darth_Poutine: Hey, can u guys take this to a private chat or to Discord? Ur filling up my screen!!!!

Painmaker: Oh, sorry. Sure.

SuicideMuffin (Guild leader): No, wait! I wanna hear what happened to Pain.

GrandAdmiralPrawn: Me too!

Darth_Poutine: OK. Sorry.

Painmaker: NP. So lately I've been noticing that my buddy liked her too…

SuicideMuffin (Guild leader): Oh, no!

Painmaker: & she seemed to dig him. They'd talk together after school. At lunch sometimes he'd leave my table to sit with her & her friends.

Painmaker: It started to drive me crazy!

DragonPrincess: Ow! Did he know that u have a crush on her?

Painmaker: I never said anything to him. I was too embarrassed…

Painmaker: But he had to know.

Painmaker: Anyway, it got to the point where I started to hate him. I mean sort of….

Painmaker: He was still my friend & we still hung out. But at times I got so angry & just wanted to hurt him.

Painmaker: A few weeks ago in gym we were playing flor hockey. He was charging toward the net full speed & I couldn't help myself. I hated him so much at that moment. I stuc

Painmaker: stuck out my leg *accidentally* & tripped him.

Painmaker: He went flying & sprained his arm. I apologized afterwards & told him I didn't mean to do it.

Painmaker: He wasn't really angry. Just said it was a boneheaded thing to do & I should be careful.

Napalmbunny78: Hey everybody, TW commands are now up. Please don't set a defensive squad without reading them.

Painmaker: But this week I found out that she agreed to go to the prom with him.

DragonPrincess: Oh, I'm so sorry Pain.

Painmaker: It felt like my heart was ripped out.

Painmaker: I was so hurt I wanted to get back at him. To hurt him, too.

Painmaker: In history class, we talked about Nelson Mandela & how he spent years in prison. The teacher asked us if we could imagine what it's like to be locked in prison, not knowin

Painmaker: knowing if u'll ever get out.

Painmaker: I couldn't help myself. I knew it was wrong, but I just couldn't stop myself.

Painmaker: I said, "Ask Joe." Every eye in the class, including hers, turned toward me. The teacher asked me what I meant.

Painmaker: My friend looked at me imploringly. But I just stared at the girl we both like & said "Ask Joe. He's been in prison. He could tell us."

DragonPrincess: Ack! U didn't!!!

Napalmbunny78 increased Count Dooku's gear to level XI

Painmaker: As soon as I said it, I hated myself for it. Joe turned white as a ghost & stared at me dumbfounded. He called me Judas & ran out of the class.

Napalmbunny78: Don't be so hard on yourself, Painmaker. Love makes you do stupid things.

Painmaker: No, Napalm, this was worse than stupid. It was unforgivable.

Painmaker: After that, I walked through the rest of the day in a daze, with that feeling u get in the pit of ur stomach when u expect the whole world to fall apart.

Painmaker: & it did.

Obiwan_Etobicoke: Sorry all. I accidentally put my NS squad in a bug zone.

Painmaker: When school was out I went over to his house to face the music. I suppose I was going to apologize, to do whatever it took to make it right.

Painmaker: But his mom said she hadn't seen or heard from him. He didn't go home that night. His mom was really worried. I had to tell her what I'd done.

Painmaker: She tore into me. "How could u? Ur his friend!" That wounded look of disappointment she gave me made me want to crawl under a rock & die.

DragonPrincess: Oh no! Where did he go?

Painmaker: The police found him early the next morning. He'd gone down near the river & slit his wrists with a razor blade. All because of me & my BFM!

DragonPrincess: OMG! Is he…

Clocktower increased General Kenobi's gear to level XIII

Napalmbunny78: Jesus!!

Painmaker: Fortunately not. He lost a lot of blood, but they found him on time.

Painmaker: I tried to visit him in the hospital, but his mother told me that he didn't want to see me. Ever again.

Painmaker: She asked me why I would do something like that to him. I couldn't answer. She told me not to call anymore & never to stop by the house again.

Painmaker: Now I found out that she's moving him to a different school yet again.

Painmaker: To top it all off, when I went back to school after a few days – I couldn't go back right away, I was too shaken – the first person I saw was her. U know, the girl.

Painmaker: She actually acknowledged my existence & spoke to me for the first time…

Painmaker: I've dreamed of that for so long! Actually talking to her…

Painmaker: Only, she looked at me with uncomprehending hatred & asked "What kind of monster are u?"

Painmaker: Had she stabbed me in the heart with a dagger she couldn't have hurt me more. Especially since she was right. I am a monster!

DragonPrincess: No, Pain! Don't say that!

Painmaker: It's true! No1 good would do that to their best friend.

Painmaker: So now, because of my own stupidity, I've lost my best friend – my only friend – & the girl who meant everything to me. Oh what an idlop

Painmaker: Idiot I am!!! I've ruined everything!

DragonPrincess: *HUG*

DragonPrincess: So what are u gonna do?

Painmaker: IDK

Painmaker: Nothing I can do. Can't go back to school.

DragonPrincess: Can u talk to someone? Ur parents?

Painmaker: Nah! My old man ran out on us when I was a kid. My mom is really lame. Doesn't get the first thing about me.

DragonPrincess: What about a teacher? A relative?

Painmaker: There's nobody.

SuicideMuffin (Guild leader): Listen Pain, you can always talk to us here.

DragonPrincess: Yes. Promise me something, Pain.

Painmaker: What?

DragonPrincess: Don't do anything stupid without talking to us first.

Painmaker: Like what?

DragonPrincess: Don't drop out of school. And for God's sake don't hurt urself.

SuicideMuffin (Guild leader): Yeah. You've done something boneheaded. But who hasn't? You're a teenager. Everyone does something dumb when they're a teen.

SuicideMuffin (Guild leader): You probably can't see it now, but in 10 yrs it won't seem as catastrophic. Trust me on this.

DragonPrincess: He's right. Don't mess ur life up because of one dumb mistake.

DragonPrincess: Promise?

Painmaker: I dunno.

DragonPrincess: Listen Pain. We care about u. Ur one of us! Please promise me ul talk to us before u do anything stupid. We're a guild. We stick together.

Painmaker: Thanks guys. I really appreciate it. U guys are the greatest.

DragonPrincess: Anytime, Pain.

SuicideMuffin (Guild leader): There's always someone here or on Discord to talk to.

Paimaker has left the guild

SuicideMuffin (Guild leader): WTF?

DragonPrincess: NOOOO!!!!!

DragonPrincess: Why did he do that? There's no way we can reach him now!

SuicideMuffin (Guild leader): I hope he's OK…

Darth_Poutine increased CT-7657 "Rex"'s gear to level XI

Obiwan_Etobicoke just promoted TIE Fighter Pilot to 7-Star

The Middle

"A story needs to have a beginning, a middle and an end," Bradley declared in an authoritative voice, with the confidence borne of his upbringing, his family's Post Road mansion near the Bridle Path, his father's status as a provincial Cabinet minister.

His audience was a small group of his classmates in a University of Toronto English Literature class gathering after their lecture at the Hart House cafeteria for a steaming cup of coffee. Since the semester had only recently begun, they were largely strangers to each other, except for Bradley and Martin, who had attended Upper Canada College together. It was three o'clock on an early January afternoon, during a heavy snowstorm. They had just tramped through the virgin snow from their classroom in the neogothic University College building, beguiled by the intoxicating freshness of the chill air, the sea of students in colourful winter coats bustling to and fro, the peerless aura of independence peculiar to undergraduates.

"*Finnegan's Wake* doesn't have any of these," he continued. "I just don't get why we have to read it. The book makes no *sense*." Across the table, Martin was enthusiastically nodding his assent, his curly nutbrown locks glistening in the light of the narrow, pointed windows beside them. His face had a dreamlike quality, as he drank in not only his mentor's words, but also the stately atmosphere of the room, its vaulted ceiling, its old-world charm. To Martin's left sat the two women of the group. Fair-haired, blue-eyed Dalia was waving to a friend at another table and signalling, with fingers to her mouth and ear, still red from the walk, that she would call later, although her eyes never strayed far from Bradley's commanding presence. Refika, a diffident, nervous young woman with short, auburn hair and dark eyes, nursed her coffee non-committally, while the fifth member of their party, bespectacled Justin, still sporting his snow-streaked, skin-tight red knit tuque, sat to Martin's right, scrolling through social media posts on his iPhone.

"It's crazy!" Martin chipped in. "The book begins in the middle of a sentence and then ends with the beginning of the *same sentence*! I mean, what was that dude *on*?" Justin pulled his nose briefly away from his screen and laughed a deep guttural laugh, before returning his attention to his Facebook feed.

Despite having appreciated the book, even if she didn't fully grasp its elusive meaning, Dalia decided that this was her opportunity to contribute to the conversation without risking her classmates' – especially Bradley's – opprobrium. "Yeah, *I'll* try some of that shit," she volunteered with exaggerated swagger, peppering her speech with an expletive that she would not ordinarily have employed if she were amongst people with whom she was fully at ease.

Bradley grinned indulgently and continued his weighty pronouncement on literature. "And the characters have to be clearly written, with distinctive, consistent personalities that the reader can connect to. Too many novels have a muddled-up, motley crew of characters that even the author seems unsure about." Bradley said this with an almost regal air, like a king addressing his countrymen, strong, authoritative, his square jaw demanding fealty.

Although she didn't fully share his perspective on literature, Dalia glanced at Bradley with admiration, before turning her attention to the tempest of wind and snow through the kaleidoscopic cut-glass window slits. "I love being warm indoors on a cold day," she said dreamily.

"Wouldn't a fire be nice on a day like this?" Martin asked, as he nibbled somewhat nervously on a blueberry muffin.

"That's a great idea!" Dalia cooed with hyperbolic brightness. "Let's chop up one of these wooden tables and make our own."

"I don't think I agree…" Refika broke in tentatively, addressing Bradley. "Life doesn't have clear beginnings and endings, so why should stories?" Her face flushed as she spoke, her voice faltering slightly on the last few words. It clearly had not been easy for her to introduce her discordant note into the conversation, conscious as she was of her strong accent, the shabbiness of her clothing compared to those of her companions.

In solidarity with Bradley, Martin dismissed her summarily. "What do you mean? Life begins with birth and ends with death. That's pretty clear."

Without looking up from his phone, Justin retorted, "Not your life, Martin. You were hatched!"

"Wow!" countered Martin, "He's actually paying attention! His girlfriend must have to blow him on Facebook in order for him to notice." Dalia winced, unable to hide her disapproval of his crude repartee. Justin threw him a dirty look.

"Well," Refika considered, uncomfortable to be the source of controversy but determined to make her case, "stories rarely encompass an entire life from birth to death…. Take my life, for example. My parents and I escaped the Bosnian genocide when I was only five years old. How do you decide when that story starts and what is back story?"

No-one spoke, sensing that Refika was not finished. She took an ample sip of her coffee, for courage rather than warmth, and continued, her voice quavering. "Does it start before the war, with my home in Sarajevo and my parents' restaurant in the old city? Or the moment the siege began? With my mother being raped before my young eyes? Or with my cousin, a seven-year-old girl, being shot dead by a sniper? It depends on the point of reference, doesn't it?"

Though delivered softly, her words had an electric impact on her classmates. Justin forsook his cellphone and peered out from under his tuque in horror. Dalia, her eyes welling with tears, was overcome by sympathy and touched Refika's sleeve in support. Uncharacteristically, Bradley was momentarily at a loss for words, and even Martin was visibly embarrassed at having chided Refika only moments earlier.

"And when does that story end?" Refika mused, still speaking quietly, tentatively, although her words carried the force of thunderclaps. "When we snuck out of our home in the dead of night, crawling on our bellies near the Miljacka River to escape detection by Serbian snipers? After we slithered through a cold, dark, unlit dirt tunnel to flee the city? When, after hiding amongst bales of hay in the back of a pick-up truck, we finally reached the border and sliced our clothing and skin against the barb-wire fences that separated us from freedom? Perhaps when we finally arrived in Canada, after many stops along the way, to begin our application for refugee status? When I finish my education and get a career of my own, start my own family? Or does it end when I can finally sleep…" her voice broke here, interrupted by a sob she could not stifle, "through the night without nightmares, without hearing the screams echoing in my head, if that ever happens?"

An awkward silence followed, as her companions grappled with the horror she had experienced. It seemed so incongruous with the splendour of Hart House, the tranquility of the lazily falling snow, the safety of Toronto. Bradley was the first to recover the power of speech. "What I meant was…." he started, but he seemed unable to complete the thought.

Amidst the din of conversation and clinking cutlery elsewhere in the cafeteria, Dalia picked up the charge, empowered by Refika's intervention to express her own dissent, although her voice quavered as she spoke. "Refika's right. Start and end points are arbitrary. But also, stories aren't always about events. They can be character studies or about emotions. These don't *need* clear narrative beginnings or endings."

"Absolutely," Refika concurred, gaining confidence by the minute, her voice steadying. "What if we wrote a story about all of us, about our discussion now?" She waved her hand around the table. "Couldn't it begin even in the middle of our conversation, at a particularly poignant juncture?"

Bradley shifted in his wooden chair. "But why would anyone want to do that?" he inquired, recovering his composure, attempting to reassert his rightful centrality to the discussion. "It's not narratively interesting. Who would want to read a story about a bunch of students – even inherently interesting ones like us – sitting in a cafeteria?"

"Sort of like a Seinfeld episode? A story about nothing?" Justin inquired.

"Because of what it says about the characters," Dalia replied to Bradley, ignoring Justin's question. "Their hopes. Their dreams. Their feelings."

"Or what it says about people in general. About humanity," Refika added.

"Exactly. I actually find simple narrative stories far less rewarding than more complex, psychological stories," Dalia attested.

"You girls sound just like Cruikshank: 'But what is the character *feeling*? What does the author want *you* to feel?'" Martin mimicked their professor's Australian accent.

"Well," Bradley conceded moodily, as he absently peeled the label off his iced tea bottle, "I see your point. But I still prefer a compelling narrative." A commotion ensued at the neighbouring table, where a woman spilled a cup of hot coffee. She and her companions began noisily cleaning it up, laughing loudly.

"Also," Refika said, taking the conversation in a different direction, "people are not clearly defined or written, as you insist they must be. They're complicated. They're not good or evil, smart or stupid. They're a jumble of feelings, emotions, inconsistencies... Take my father, for example. He was a victim of hatred, intolerance and genocide in Bosnia. Yet, for some reason that I will never understand, he collects paraphernalia from Nazi Germany."

Dalia gasped, her hands grasping the edge of the table. Martin let out a low whistle. Justin, who by this time had put his cellular phone aside, exclaimed, "You've got to be kidding!"

"Uniforms, posters, medals, flags," Refika continued. "I've told him time and time again that if you oppose genocide, it's wrong to idolize a regime that committed genocide against others. Yet, I can't get through to him. His behaviour disgusts me, but he's still my father and I still love him.... Are either of us clear characters?"

Still clutching the table, Dalia said plaintively, "My grandmother is a Holocaust survivor...."

Refika looked pained. "I'm so sorry, Dalia. I didn't know that. I didn't mean to upset you," she said. "Please understand that I am so embarrassed by his collection."

Dalia didn't know how to respond and fell silent. After a while she said, "She was in a concentration camp toward the end of the war. When the Nazis abandoned the camp to escape the oncoming American army, her mother told her to hide in the camp latrines – *inside* what they used as a toilet, you understand – to escape the forced death march to another camp. She remained there, buried up to her neck in human waste, until she was rescued, but she never saw any of her family again.... They were all murdered." She paused, then added harshly, "How *anyone* can collect Nazi memorabilia is beyond me. It's *inexcusable!*"

"I'm not arguing, Dalia. I... I agree with you. Completely. But he's my *father*. What am I to do?" Refika chided herself inwardly for speaking too freely, revealing too much. She did not know these classmates well enough to open up as she had.

"No, I'm not blaming *you*, Refika. It must be tough for you," Dalia said. She stared at her hands uncomfortably. Then, to defuse the tension, she declared, "But I suppose that just goes to prove your point that human beings are mighty complicated. So why make literary characters straightforward?"

"I guess… I guess you have a point," Bradley said weakly. The conversation had taken a turn that made him ill at ease. No longer was he in control, the star, as he usually was in all settings. Instead, he was on his heels, uncertain. Both Martin and Dalia seemed surprised, disappointed by his growing hesitancy. Refika, however, noticed this change with growing excitement, for the first time finding him vulnerable, human, *cute*. As their discussion continued, she found herself unable to take her eyes off him, discovering in his discomfort the mystique that others responded to in his dominance.

"Wow, this conversation has gotten real heavy all of the sudden," Justin observed. "Lighten up, dudes! Anyone seen any good movies lately?"

At first, no-one felt comfortable discussing something so trivial after the painful revelations they had heard, so the table fell silent once again. After a short pause, however, Martin responded, "I saw *War Horse* last weekend. It was pretty good for a movie about a horse."

Justin said, "I saw *Girl with the Dragon Tattoo*. That was *cool!*"

"Ooh! Daniel Craig is really sexy!" Dalia added, regaining her composure.

"Oh, come on!" Martin shouted. "He's got to be the worst Bond *ever*."

"*I* don't think so," Bradley disagreed in a measured tone. "I actually think he's pretty good."

"Well, okay," Martin backtracked. "He's not terrible, but he's no Sean Connery."

"Hey, I heard U2's coming to Toronto this summer," Justin announced. Then lifting his face skyward, he bellowed, "God, if you actually exist and are listening, I'd really love a pair of tickets."

"Oh, I'm sure God's got nothing better to do than conjure up concert tickets for you, buddy," Martin snapped.

"Wouldn't it be sweet, though?" Justin mused.

"I don't know…. U2 would be alright, but I'd rather see someone cool, like Alice in Chains or Cage the Elephant," Dalia responded.

"Wow!" said Martin, "You really like your music on the edge."

"What about you, Bradley? Do you have any strong opinions on music, or do you save that for literature?" Justin asked cheekily.

Bradley shrugged. "I think I'm better off leaving well enough alone." He said with an impish grin. "I do like Foo Fighters, though…."

When the great wall clock struck a quarter to four, Refika, who had been quiet during the latter part of the conversation, gathered her belongings and announced that she had a four-o'clock class at Sid Smith and needed to depart. Before taking her leave, however, she scribbled her number on a slip of paper and thrust it toward Bradley, whom she clearly caught off guard.

"So is this the end of our story, Bradley, or is it just the beginning?" she teased, a mischievous smile enveloping her enigmatic face. With that, she strode directly to the exit without looking back.

The Siren's Call

Matthew's world was upended early one evening in suburban Philadelphia, while traipsing through the neighbourhood with his wife. For several months, they had adopted the habit of walking together after work, when their schedules permitted. It afforded them the opportunity to enjoy a little fresh air and attempt to reconnect with each other. With the demands of their careers, raising their three children and caring for his wife's elderly parents, these strolls were an island of tranquility in a far too stormy sea.

On this particular May evening, they were debating the relative merits of Leonard Cohen and Bob Dylan, who had recently been awarded the Nobel Prize for literature. As a transplanted Canadian, Matthew believed that Cohen did not get the respect he merited in the US, whereas Dylan was overvalued. His American wife viewed the matter differently. It was the kind of conversation they had together lately – distant, cold, clinical.

"I just don't think he deserved the Nobel Prize. His songs are tremendous, but I think Leonard Cohen's lyrics are more literary, more evocative," Matthew expounded, sweat beading up on his pimply scalp beneath his thinning ginger hair, as they ambled along a street dominated by red maples, oaks and cherry trees on ample, luscious lawns. The weather was perfect and, with the lengthening days, the evening was still bright and sunny, though not as hot and humid as it would become in June.

"Dylan had a more profound and enduring impact on song writing than Cohen. All the greats – Lou Reed, Springsteen, Tom Petty, John Mellencamp, Melissa Etheridge – trace their craft to the doors that Dylan kicked open. Don't get me wrong. Leonard Cohen is great in his own right, but just hasn't had that same impact," his wife argued, her green eyes fixed on the road in front of her severe black walking shoes. They turned onto a private street with no sidewalk, so they had to tread cautiously on the road. The street was on a downslope, with majestic trees towering overhead dripping curtains of leaves between them and the clouds high above, allowing patches of azure sky to peek out here and there. The effect of the contrasting hues, textures, and depths was breathtaking.

"No argument. But a Nobel Prize in literature is for, oh I don't know, *literature*. Not song writing. Leonard Cohen was an accomplished poet, who published many volumes of his excellent poetry. Dylan was a songwriter only," he rejoined, as he took in the delicate scent of a lilac bush, the visual symphony of a cherry tree in bloom, the countless other delights of springtime in the Main Line neighbourhood.

They arrived at an intersection of two small suburban streets. After crossing, they branched off to the right and were able to rejoin a sidewalk. At that point, Matthew's eyes were riveted to an ostensibly trivial and mundane event. Across the street, a young woman, about thirty years of age, emerged from the side door of a well-maintained ranch-style house, its lawn beautifully-manicured, carrying some sporting equipment – a tennis racquet, a football, other sundry items – to a metallic blue SUV in the driveway. A shock of wavy blonde hair fell to just below her exquisite, bare shoulders. He marked her lightly-tanned skin, her elegant arms, her flawless neck framed by a crisp white tank top, the form-fitting sky blue Capri pants descending to her shapely, muscular calves, below which she was barefoot. Mostly, he was arrested by her bearing, which married the freshness and beauty of youth with the assurance of an adult. Each step she took toward the vehicle displayed a grace and vigour that was at once poetic and divine.

The effect this apparition had on Matthew was immediate and overwhelming. He felt the earth shaking beneath his feet, experienced a fleeting sensation of falling. That gave way to a sharp pang in the pit of his stomach, a powerful longing, a staggering, unexplainable sense of loss. The contrast between that fresh, taut young woman and his middle-aged wife was unbearably heart-breaking for him. He was moved almost to tears.

Nevertheless, he had the presence of mind not to raise his wife's ire by gawking. Instead, he continued their conversation without missing a beat, forcing his eyes back to his wife and the sidewalk ahead, so as to obscure from her the profound disturbance in his soul. All the while, he fixed the young woman through the corner of his eye – devoured all he could of her – until the progress of their strides pushed her outside his field of vision. They continued walking until they reached the end of the block, then veered right onto a small street shielded by a vast overhang of trees with dense foliage towering over the road, filtering out the sky. A crimson cardinal flew across their path, casting a quizzical look in their direction, before ascending to the verdant, multilayered arboreal canopy above.

Matthew kept his part of the conversation up amiably, but his mind was riveted to the image of that young woman, which he replayed in his head unceasingly. In response to a point his wife was making, he heard himself produce a suitably urbane, literate reply, "Not only that, but Dylan is nasty. His songs are designed to hurt. How can you compare a song like *Positively Fourth Street* or *Masters of War*, where he acidly calls for his target's death in the most brutal way, to Leonard Cohen at his nastiest in *Famous Blue Raincoat*? Even at his darkest, Cohen talks about forgiveness."

His wife, oblivious to his unrest, countered, "Dylan's anger is a core element of his poetry. He's angry at the system, angry at the mealy-mouthed false liberals, angry at all those who enable injustice. And he uses his craftily chosen lyrics to expose them, to skewer them. Admit it, Matthew, you're just partial to Cohen and Joni Mitchell because they're Canadian." She fixed him with one of her corporate boardroom glances, part smile, part triumphant snarl.

He wondered what it said about him that he was in complete inner turmoil, but could carry on without a ripple on the surface. Surely that was not to his credit, he thought guiltily. Could he do the same if he were to have an affair? If he were to murder someone?

In the end, as they approached the red brick façade of their colonial at the end of their promenade, he offered her a concession of sorts. "Well, I guess you're right, in a way. Dylan is more widely recognized, more iconic than Cohen. But I still don't see his songs as literature." They unlocked the stained walnut front door and entered the house.

That night, sleep proved elusive, as he obsessed over the image, puzzling over it, pining over it. When he did finally drift off to sleep, it was fitful, punctuated by troubling dreams. In one, his first girlfriend, from college, set fire to an empty coffin. When he asked her whose it was, she laughed cruelly and snapped, "Don't you know?" In another, he wandered through an old house – perhaps his childhood home? – frantically searching for something. But the house was empty, sinister, foreboding. He awoke in a panic.

It was still dark. Almost two hours before the alarm would ring. He tried to take stock, to make sense of it all. *What can it possibly mean? I'm a fifty-year-old man mooning over a woman half my age,* he thought to himself. *So she was gorgeous. That's really no excuse.* Then he wondered, *Was she truly that pretty? My eyes are no longer what they used to be, and I was only able to catch a fleeting glimpse of her.... Oh, but what does it matter? I'm happily married. I love my wife and my family. I don't even know that woman. She's just an idea, a concept; she's not real. So why does she affect me so? Why can't I get her out of my head?*

Birds started to chirp outside the window. *It's not like I haven't felt something like this before. But it's been so long – before I was married. It's like the futility of boyhood puppy love, when you're too young to do anything about it but moon. Only now there's no point because I'm too old. My die is already cast. We're strange creatures,* he mused. *When we're young, we can't wait to be older. We spend the rest of our lives wishing we were younger. Is there ever a point when we're happy in our own skins?*

He recalled the lyric of a Blue Rodeo song, about life passing the singer by. *Is that all this is? Mid-life blues?* He sneered at the idea, as it trivialized his profound agitation. *No,* he thought, *it's just the drip-drip dreariness of life that's sapping my energy, my enthusiasm…*

Eventually, he drifted off again and slept fitfully until the alarm sounded.

In the late afternoon, after work, he collected his twins from school. His son sat behind him, his daughter on the passenger's side of the rear seat of his sedan.

"What happened at school today, monsters?" he asked with forced joviality. "Did you have a good day?"

"Great!" replied his son with enthusiasm, "Mr. Burton wasn't there today, so we had extra gym instead of Math!"

"That's exactly why we send you to school," he snapped back, "*Not* to be educated!" He turned his attention to his daughter in the offset rectangle of the rear-view mirror. "And what about you, Jody? You seem awfully quiet."

"I want to quit soccer, Daddy," she said pensively.

"What? I thought you loved soccer?"

"Well, Ms. Martinson made me a sub. I won't even get to *play* on Sunday," Jody complained.

"I'm sorry, Sweetie. Don't give up, though. Just because you're a sub doesn't mean you won't play. Subs get into the game, just later, when they can have the greatest impact," he tried to reassure her.

"Oh, Daddy!" she cried, "Don't be so naïve!"

He was taken aback. "That's a pretty big word for a nine-year-old. Where did you learn it?"

"From Jimmy Benson at choir practice. He said it was naïve to believe in the tooth fairy," she stated matter-of-factly.

"Well, this isn't like the tooth fairy. I'm sure you're gonna play on Sunday. Just keep practising and give it a chance," he retorted, trying not to smile condescendingly.

While Jody was considering this, her brother chimed in, "You mean the tooth fairy isn't real? Then who puts the dollar bills under our pillows?"

"Santa Claus...." Matthew muttered under his breath. He would need to work hard to keep up with these two. His ascendancy would not last long.

He drove the same route he always took but, about midway, he surrendered to an inescapable impulse to detour past her house. He glanced quickly at the house, the driveway where his equilibrium had been shattered, but there was no sign either of her or the SUV. He chastised himself, *Honestly, you're acting like a teenager! And with your children in the car, too!*

"Did you get lost again, Daddy? This isn't the way home!" his son chided him with narrowed eyes.

"Oops! I guess I made a wrong turn," he replied, using his notoriously poor sense of direction as cover.

"Boy, Daddy. Wait 'til we tell Mommy. *She* never gets lost!"

"Well, *she* never takes you for frozen yogurt after practice either, does she?" he responded flippantly.

"Alright!" the twins exclaimed in unison. They were growing up quickly, but at least he could still rely on his bag of tricks to remain the cool dad. As he parked outside the frozen yogurt retailer, he promised himself that he wouldn't drive by that house again. At least not with his children....

His wife arrived home very late that evening – too late for their walk – and in a bear of a mood. It happened with increasing frequency of late.

"Couldn't you have given the kids dinner?" It was more a death sentence than a question.

"You didn't ask me to," he responded, expecting the wrath of the tempest. "Today's not usually *my* day."

"I shouldn't *need* to ask! Why can't you think of anyone but your*self*? If I'm not home for our walk, you've got to figure I'm running late and need you to help out," she snapped.

He didn't want to escalate, so he lowered his ruddy head and apologized, the Canadian in him ready to compromise. "I'm sorry, Penny. I didn't think. Look, I can throw some hotdogs in the broiler quickly."

"No, you *didn't* think. I wish you *would* think about someone other than yourself for a change," she piled on, with venom, the veins in her temples bulging beneath her salt-and-pepper pixie cut.

After a short silence, however, she spoke in a less harsh, more laboured tone. "No," she said, visibly trying to reign in her anger, "I shouldn't snap like that. I'm just under a lot of stress with this merger. I *do* wish you'd help me out a bit more, though." The health care insurance company she worked for was being bought over by a rival. As head of Human Resources, she was involved in the negotiations to transition from two companies to one, which would involve numerous layoffs. She bore a heavy burden of guilt.

As he withdrew to the kitchen, Penny called after him, "Don't worry about Matt. He's not coming home til later." His older son, Matthew Jr., his namesake, had turned fifteen and was never at home anymore, rarely had time for the family. It upset Matthew, but he acknowledged that American teenagers had much more independence than he'd had growing up in Vancouver. They also were over-burdened with extracurricular activities – soccer practice, band practice, the track team. He doubted that it was for the better, but Penny insisted it was appropriate, and they couldn't raise him too much differently from his friends.

While he removed the hotdogs and some frozen soup from the freezer, he reflected on the changes that had overtaken his wife in recent years. Not only was she older, flabbier, greyer – the obvious, superficial gifts of Father Time – but she had also become more irritable, less attentive, less affectionate. She lost her temper incessantly, always with an excuse: stress at work, her mother's illness, a headache. At the same time, she had become less adventurous, less fun-loving. In the early years, they had travelled widely – to sub-Saharan Africa, the Australian outback, the Andes, wherever the whim had taken them. Now, she was more sedentary, finding excuses not to travel, not to venture out on weekends, preferring to remain at home with her kids. He hadn't thought much about it before, but she was no longer the woman he married.

To be fair, he considered, she would have similar complaints about him. Although he tried to keep in shape, he didn't look like he did twenty years ago. He snored at night, making it hard for her to get a decent night's sleep. That didn't help her mood either. He often got too involved in his work and was a little self-centred. And he *could* do more to help with the twins. That was the crux of the problem, he judged. A marriage that had bristled with energy, with passion, had lost its urgency, its fire, its focus, as time waved its perverse wand and transformed them from princes into toads. It was unnatural, he reflected, to mate for life. Humans were among the few species that did so.

An image floated through his mind. They were on a boat in the Galapagos, traveling from one island to another, early in their marriage. The boat hurtled through the Pacific at breakneck speed, lurching and plummeting on each enormous wave with an earth-splitting THUMP, the boat convulsing in tremors. They wondered nervously whether the rickety boat could withstand the immense force, or whether it would shatter, plunging them into a watery grave. With the scorching sun above, the saltwater splashing in, the cool spray in her sunbleached hazelnut hair, the unquenchable light in her emerald eyes, her drenched t-shirt hugging each fulsome curve of her young body, the thrill was absolute. They kissed each other fiercely, urgently. Oblivious to the danger, the other passengers, the captain cheering them on in Spanish over his microphone. That was how it was in the early years.

Of course, they still loved each other, he reflected. But love is a word with too many meanings. In the early years, their love was elemental. They loved each other like the wind. Like a raging fire. As if life itself depended on their love. Now their love was more commodified, transactional. Like a comfortable pair of shoes, a bowl of soup, an old, worn sweater.

Once dinner was ready, he called the family to the table.

The following afternoon, abandoned again by Penny, he decided to walk alone. With his soul in deepening turmoil, he trudged distractedly, head down, oblivious to the rabbit eyeing him warily across a lawn, the splendour of the cherry tree blossoms, the cool scented breeze that wafted through the nascent foliage. The myriad sumptuous pleasures of the season held no attraction for him.

Without consciously planning a route, his feet carried him inevitably, a lemming to the cliff, to *her* street, *her* house, *her* driveway. He drank in the long expanse of the house, the rectangular windows of the converted garage, the black trim of the postern from which she had danced into his brain. Yet again, there was no sign of her or the SUV. Had he just imagined her?

In utter confusion, he crossed the street toward the house, failing to notice an oncoming bicycle, which swerved to avoid him. "Sorry!" he called out in surprise, in embarrassment, to the angry cyclist. Standing on her driveway, the driveway where it happened, he noticed a small rectangular package in the bushes. It looked like a box of cheques that the mail carrier might have dropped on his route. On impulse, he picked it up and read the label. Mr. D. Jackson. Was that her husband? Her father? Before he understood what he was doing, he was marching up the flagstone path to the front door, package in hand, pressing the doorbell. His legs trembled, his breath fluttered, as he waited for her to appear. *What am I doing*, he asked himself. *Have I lost my mind?*

At first, there was no response. *No-one's home*, Matthew thought with relief. *I'll just leave it and go.* Soon, however, the shifting kaleidoscopic patterns of light and shadows through the glazed sidelight indicated that someone was approaching. Matthew could hardly breathe. He heard someone adjust the chain and a male voice called out, "Yes, who is it?"

On the verge of panic, Matthew sputtered through his crooked incisors, "Ah... I, uh... It's a package...."

A dark-haired teenage boy opened the door and looked at Matthew quizzically. *Who was he? Her brother? Her son?* Matthew didn't see any resemblance between them, although, in truth, he had not had a good enough look at her in the first place. In his disappointment, he recovered a modicum of his composure and said, "Someone dropped this package for you on the road. I thought I'd make sure you got it."

The boy took the box and thanked him. As he was closing the door, Matthew peered intently behind him, but there was no sign of her. Completely discomposed, he hastily retreated down the path to the sidewalk, at once relieved and deflated.

What utter insanity, he berated himself. *What were you thinking? What's wrong with you? This has to stop now!* He returned home directly, with quick strides, promising himself that he would not return to that house.

A few nights later, he woke up from a vivid dream. He was standing on a pier fishing in a mountain stream with *her*, the blonde young woman from the driveway. All at once, there was a powerful tug on his line and he lost his balance, falling into the stream. She laughed merrily while he struggled with a powerful undertow. The last thing he remembered before waking was wondering in bitter astonishment, "Why is she laughing? Can't she see that I'm drowning?"

How long can this go on? he wondered as he lay awake in the pre-dawn. He hadn't slept well in days. He was distracted at work. *It's madness! It can't be about her. How could it be? I've never even met her! It has to be about something deeper.* An owl hooted from a tree outside.

All the wasted time, he suddenly lamented, with the sharp clarity that only comes at night, *all the paths not taken*. There was so much that he had wanted to do with his life that had gotten lost over the years. Chief among them was travel. In the early years, he and Penny had often talked about living overseas in an exotic locale, perhaps the Amazon rainforest. The romantic appeal of reinventing himself on another continent, in another language, another culture, enthralled him. He had also been eager to write. His computer was a graveyard of forgotten story ideas that never came to fruition. He was certain he had a novel in him, if he could devote the time to it. But there never was time. Between work and family obligations, there were always reasons not to. And, truth be told, whenever there was time, he had squandered it, like so much sand beneath his feet.

He glanced at his wife, sleeping soundly beside him, illuminated by the errant rays of a streetlamp through a crack in the Venetian blind. Her steady intakes of breath sent his thoughts in a different direction as the night wore on. Who was this woman he shared a bed with, he wondered. She bore some resemblance to the girl he had married, but time shifts and distorts everything, even love. "What am I even doing here?" he whispered softly to himself, "I don't belong here." As if in response, Penny shifted in her sleep, then settled, her breathing steady again. A Canadian in the land of Trump. That was something he could never stomach. Penny was no Trump supporter – far from it – but in the end, Trump was still her president. Some of their friends had even voted for him. Matthew could never reconcile that. He would always be a foreigner, an outsider.

It was as if the image of the young woman in her Capri pants had breached the dyke, freeing the tides of dissatisfaction to ravage his soul. In his late middle age, he now realized all he had squandered, all his regrets, his failures, how far he was from home.

The following morning, Matthew sat at his desk in his office, unable to concentrate on work as advertising director for a sub-urban Philadelphia weekly newspaper. The deadline for the next edition was that afternoon, but he couldn't focus on the layouts that his assistant proposed. Instead, he thought of Penny, the way she used to be and how she behaved now. How empty his life had become! How much more he had wanted from it. Absentmind-edly, he Googled flights to Brazil.

I can't continue the way I am, he decided at last. *I need to make a change. If I don't do it now, I never will. It'll be too late.* He lifted the phone to call his wife, but stopped mid-dial. *What's the use? What would I say anyway?* Instead, he buzzed his secretary, telling her that he was under the weather and would leave for home early. His assistant could close off the ads this week. He glanced forlornly around his office, the framed prints, the binders full of leads on the sparse shelves, before departing. *Is this all I've accom-plished with my life?* Carrying his briefcase, he rode the elevator to the underground parking lot. After retrieving his car, he drove directly to the airport.

When he didn't arrive for their afternoon walk, Penny dialed his cellphone, but was transferred directly to voicemail. Immediately, she began to worry. She had witnessed his agita-tion for days, felt the storm brewing within him. *I know I've been difficult, what with work and all. And it's not just work,* she admitted to herself. *I've gotten so irritable lately. I don't know why, but I can't help it. It's just that I feel so tired, so drained, so.... It's all so dreary.... I guess it's just a change of life. Time really does a number on us! But I'm sure it happens to everybody. We're not unique. We should be able to deal with it. But the truth is, we've never been good at talking about our problems. We just keep them bottled up and try to put up a good front.*

She called him repeatedly all evening, to no avail, her anxiety rising. *Should I call the police? This isn't like him. No, perhaps not yet.... He'll turn up. Honestly, why does he have to be such a child? Why can't he accept that we all get old, that life can't be what it was when we were younger? If only he opened up a bit more, instead of pulling a stupid stunt like this....* She put the twins to bed and returned to her vigil in front of the living room window, telephone clutched tightly in hand.

At eleven o'clock that night, Matthew emerged through the front door of his Main Line home, dripping with rain, a serious expression on his face. More worried than angry, Penny asked, "Where *were* you? I've been calling you for *hours*!"

"I've been out. Thinking...." he replied somberly. "At the airport."

"The airport!" she exclaimed, "What's going on with you, Matthew?"

"It's just...." he started, but seemed to lose his power of speech. After a short pause, he tried again, "It's just that I need to make some changes."

"What kind of changes?" his wife asked, a lump in her throat.

He stared at her uneasily, something between a smirk and a scowl on his lips. Then, bending slowly, he pulled a cork-covered writer's notebook out of a bag he retrieved from his rain-streaked briefcase. "Well," he said, a little self-conscious, "to begin with, it's time I started writing. I... I don't know if I'll be any good, but I certainly can try."

She was about to laugh, when the earnestness of his expression convinced her to restrain herself. "That's a good idea," she said.

"We also need to plan some travel. I don't mean a weekend in the Poconos. I mean *real* travel. Like we used to. Maybe Brazil." His face was intense, his round blue eyes defiant. She studied them carefully before replying.

"OK," she said at last. "It *has* been too long since we went somewhere exciting. Maybe that's just what we need."

He relaxed visibly and put his briefcase down, still keeping his distance from her.

"Let's go to bed, Honey. It's been a long day," she implored him.

"You go, Penny. I'm going to start writing first. I'll join you later."

That night, he sat at the dining room table, pen in hand, a snifter of whiskey at the ready. He listened intently to the metronome of the old grandfather clock, the rain rattling the house's old windows, the echoes of all that was no more, that would never be again. *We can't run away from our choices*, he thought. *There's no point. And it's too late to start again. Too many entangled webs keep us where we are. All we can do is carry on the best we can, hoping not to get crushed under their immense weight.* He sighed a melancholy sigh, answered from without by a loud peal of thunder, the heavy patter of the rain. Taking a draught of the whiskey, he began scribbling in his notebook.

Speculation

"Are you ready yet?" Henry asked.

The tall, round-faced teen's impatience was palpable, his thick rubicund lips twitching in anticipation. The last bell had rung over ten minutes earlier, and he was bursting at the seams to get going. Yet his scrawny, shorter friend was only now fiddling with the lock on his locker in the hallway of Harbord Collegiate high school, binder in hand, still without his coat and boots.

"Sorry about that. I'm going as fast as I can," Simon assured him, scowling at a reddish, translucent acne pimple on his nose with the aid of a small rectangular mirror he had affixed to the outside of his locker door.

"Well, what took you so long?"

"I was talking to Debbie Bender. *Debbie Bender*, asshole!" Simon exclaimed triumphantly, his entire face beaming like a harvest moon. "She's the whole reason I signed up for French this semester."

"Sweet! You'll have to tell me about it. But not now! It's the first Friday of the month!" his friend chided him.

Simon quickly donned his winter gear, slammed his locker door, snapped the lock and raced his friend to the bus shelter at the corner of Harbord and Bathurst, where they waited to board the Bathurst streetcar southbound to Queen Street West. The two grade 11 classmates collected superhero comic books and today – the first Friday of November 1983 – was the day for their monthly pilgrimage to the comic stores in downtown Toronto.

Their first stop was the Silver Snail, a large store with a black sign on the south side of Queen Street, W., just east of Spadina. The store owner, who knew them as regulars, greeted them as they entered. They rushed to the shelves displaying the recently published comic books, before diving into the wooden bins that occupied the bulk of the store containing carefully preserved back issues. The store was a sensory experience. The brightly coloured cover art displayed throughout the store, the sweet, musty odour of old comics, the rock music playing in the background, the crisp feel of the well-preserved magazines in their feverish fingers.

The boys preferred Marvel comics over their better-established rival, DC. Henry's favorites were the *X-Men*, *The Incredible Hulk*, and *Fantastic Four* series, whereas Simon specialized in *The Amazing Spiderman*, his absolute favourite, as well as *The Avengers*, and the *What If* specialty series. They each selected one or two enticing back issues to augment their collection and proceeded to the cash.

Their ritual concluded with a visit to Dragon Lady Comics, on the north side of Queen Street, closer to University. Although the Silver Snail was larger, the boys loved this shop more, with its sweet, welcoming smell, its friendly manager, and its rogue's gallery of rare and expensive comics hanging on the wall behind the cash. Simon stared up enviously at *Iron Man* #1, *The Amazing Spiderman* #1 and *Fantastic Four* #3, all in near mint condition, each priced at over a thousand dollars. But what really made him salivate, was a copy of *Amazing Fantasy* #15, on sale for eighteen hundred dollars. If Dragon Lady was Simon's temple, this was its sacred relic.

He tugged on Henry's arm excitedly. "That... that's like the first ever appearance of Spiderman! What I'd give for that, man!"

"Keep dreaming. You'd have to save your babysitting and paper-route money for years to be able to afford that," Henry reasoned, with his ever-present, easy smile.

"Aw man, wouldn't it be sweet, though?" Simon mused, his intense azure eyes boring a hole through the prized comic.

They rummaged through the bins, selecting more affordable additions to their collections. Simon pulled out a few back issues of the *Amazing Spiderman* from the early 1970s in good condition for between three to five dollars each. Henry chose an early *Daredevil* for six dollars and an *Avengers* issue from the same era in very good condition for five dollars. Then they pulled out a few of the new comics that had just hit the stores, before heading to the cash.

As they were paying, the boys struck up a conversation with the store's affable manager about the comic world, like they always did.

"Hey, will you boys be here next month?" the manager asked.

"Yeah, the first Friday, like always," Henry replied.

"You've got to get your hands on the new *Thor* that's arriving then. It's gonna be *huge*," the manager promised. He always tried to pass on the latest news and comic-collecting scuttlebutt to his good customers.

"Really? What the big deal?" Henry inquired.

"Walt Simonson is taking over the series. That'll make it pretty valuable, sort of like the Miller *Daredevils*. The first one, in particular, could go through the roof." Simonson was a highly regarded artist. Comics drawn by him were prized by collectors, who drove their prices up considerably. When another famed artist, Frank Miller, took over the *Daredevil* series a few years earlier, #158's market value jumped from its cover price of forty cents to over sixty dollars in a matter of months.

Henry whistled. "We'll be here. Save one for each of us."

"If it's going to be even half as big as I think it'll be, you might want to grab as many as you can," the manager advised.

"Thanks for the tip. See you next month," Henry said, as they paid for their comics and left the store.

On the streetcar home, Henry, always the schemer, couldn't stop talking about the manager's advice.

"Man, that sounds like a can't miss," he mused, his tongue slowly, deliberately moistening his thick underlip.

Simon was less enthusiastic. "I dunno, Henry. I never liked *Thor*. I don't think I want to bother." Simon was a purist. He collected comics because he loved them, not as an investment. To be sure, he was hoping that his collection would appreciate in value and one day be worth a fortune, like the early DC *Superman* comics of the late 1930s and early 1940s. But he never envisioned selling them, debasing them by treating them as a mere asset. If he wasn't interested in a series, that was the end of the story.

"Aw, c'mon, asshole! How can you pass up a deal like this? As my old man says, 'when opportunity knocks, open the damn door!'"

"What's the point? I'd rather spend my money on something I want to read. Something I'll be proud to have in my collection," Simon declared, knitting his pale eyebrows together.

"Boy, are you thick!" Henry taunted. Standing in the aisle of the bus, his tall, hulking frame would have appeared menacing, but for his incongruous, impish smile. "When you make a killing on this, you can use your profits to buy something you'd *really* like to own. Just think of it. If this jumps as fast as the first Miller *Daredevil*, it could be worth $50 by the new year. If you buy five, you could make a profit of two hundred and fifty big ones!"

"I suppose...." Simon conceded. "I guess I could buy one and see what happens."

"Ah, you're *hopeless*, man! Like the Chocolate Bullfrogs say, *don't walk through the front door only to run screaming from the back!*"

Simon was unclear on the relevance of his friend's quotation and was about to challenge him. They were approaching Simon's stop, however, so he pulled the grey cord to signal the driver and bade his friend goodbye before exiting through the rear doors when the bus squeaked to a halt.

As soon as Simon got home, he secluded himself in the bedroom he shared with his younger brother and inspected his purchases. First, he carefully leafed through the latest issues that had just hit the stands to verify that they hadn't been damaged in transit. He then inserted them in clear plastic bags to protect them from scratches and humidity, carefully pressing out the air and taping the bag's folded-over edges. Next, he turned his attention to his prizes: the vintage issues from the 1970s. They were sold in bags, so he looked over the front and back covers through their protective sleeves to ascertain their condition and ensure that they were well-preserved.

These preliminaries taken care of, Simon now settled into the joyous main attraction; he would read one of his new treasures. He selected *Amazing Spiderman* #89, the one that excited him most. With great anticipation, he cautiously peeled the adhesive tape off the bag and gently removed the magazine, placing it on the faux cedar pressed board desk, and inhaled deeply, revelling in the aroma of old paper. First, he admired the cover art, three narrow panels depicting a battle between Spidey and Doc Ock near the roof of an apartment building, framed against a bright yellow background, with the black-and-white caption, "DOC OCK LIVES!" He gingerly turned the pages, careful not to fold them or otherwise put pressure on the spine. Then he absorbed the story frame-by-frame, studying the artwork and following the footnotes that explained anomalies and kept track of developments in previous issues and other titles. When he finished, he read it a second time before carefully returning it to its bag and sealing it anew.

It was a religious experience for Simon. Every Tuesday afternoon after school, Simon attended a Hebrew evening school in North York, where he learned about Jewish tradition and scriptures. On Saturday mornings, his father brought him to synagogue at the Holy Blossom Temple. But none of that meant anything to Simon. *These* were his Bible, his Talmud, the most precious of all worldly artifacts.

As he carefully filed his new additions alphabetically and numerically into the long, rectangular cardboard boxes that housed his collection and slid the boxes safely into the back of his closet, he reflected once more on the shopkeeper's advice. *It would cheapen all this*, he thought. *It's not worth it.*

When they returned to Queen Street the next month Henry made a beeline for the new magazines' shelf at the Silver Snail, but found the *Thor* slot empty. Perplexed and slightly annoyed, he marched directly to the manager.

"Hey, where are the new *Thors*?" he asked breathlessly.

"Oh, you guys are about a week too late. The demand has been through the roof! We sold out as soon as it hit the stands," the manager responded.

Henry whistled through his puffy lips. "You're kidding!" he said in amazement.

"We should be getting more in, but the price has already jumped to $15."

"Already? Only a week after its release?" Simon was dumbfounded.

"I'm as surprised as you are," the manager admitted. "I've never seen anything like it. If it keeps up, it could hit $50 by next month!"

"Any idea where we can get our hands on it?" Henry pressed.

"Well, I shouldn't really say this, but you can try Dragon Lady down the block. I'm sure they've sold out too, though."

Henry's face fell. "Damn! I guess we missed out," he lamented.

They skipped their traditional rummage through the store and bolted to Dragon Lady, running nearly all the way. Henry was buoyed by the unlikely hope that they could still buy a few copies. Simon, who had no interest in purchasing the issue, was still eager to see the comic that generated such demand. Once at the store, a quick glance at the new comics shelf dashed what little hope Henry had of striking treasure: the *Thor* shelf was vacant. The boys exchanged disappointed glances. They approached the store manager, who was filing first series *Ghost Rider* issues in the back, and asked him about the new *Thor*.

"You won't believe this, but we sold out the day it hit the stand. That's never happened before," he told them. "We've actually gotten a new shipment in this morning, but they're selling for $13.50 already."

"That's just crazy!" Henry sputtered. "So we're outta luck."

"Not quite," said the manager with a toothy grin. "I knew you two'd be in this week, so I put one away for each of you before it sold out. They're yours at the regular price, if you want 'em."

The boys were overwhelmed with gratitude. "You're the greatest!" Henry gushed, his customary grin returning to his face.

"Thanks a million!" Simon added warmly.

The manager walked with them to the front cash, where he pulled out two comic books from a counter drawer. The boys inhaled deeply, momentously, as they got their first look at Simonson's powerful cover. Against a white background, a large muscle-bound brown creature wearing Thor's royal blue armour, yellow boots, white winged helmet and crimson cape was swinging the mighty hammer Mjölnir in a downward arc. In its seismic wake, the Thor series masthead and the Marvel Thor icon that grace the top of every *Thor* issue were shattered and disarrayed, sweeping off the edge of the cover. The artwork had a grace and fluidity that conveyed power and motion in a manner so vivid that Simon had not seen in any other comic before. It was cover art that would be imitated often in the future, but never equalled. It filled him with awe and wonder, stunned him into a silent reverie.

"This is incredible! Is there any way we can get our hands on more of these?" Henry asked rapaciously.

The manager rubbed his cleft chin thoughtfully with the tip of his right forefinger. "I suppose you can try convenience stores. And maybe.... No. Well, maybe even supermarkets and book-stores. They don't buy large numbers like we do, and they don't order all titles like comic shops do. But they *do* sometimes carry comics and may get one or two *Thors* in their monthly shipment. It's worth a try anyway."

Simon stared up from the glorious cover art to his holy grail, the copy of *Amazing Fantasy* #15 on the wall, as a powerful idea came over him. What if he could find twenty copies of *Thor* #337? He could then wait a few short months until it hit $100, as it seemed destined to do, and then sell them all. That would give him enough money to buy the comic of his dreams. That wouldn't be a betrayal of the beauty of comic collecting, he rea-soned, since he wasn't doing it for something so base as money. He was doing it to adorn his collection with the most perfect comic ever published.

"That's a *great* idea!" Simon chirped, his voice rising with genuine enthusiasm.

"Could we also buy a couple of the copies you're selling for $13.50?" Henry inquired.

"Of course," the manager replied. "Even at that price, you can't go wrong. It's bound to jump in value."

The boys each bought three copies at the higher price, in addition to the ones the manager sold them at the cover price.

For the next three weeks, as soon as school was out, the two friends travelled by TTC to different parts of the city, searching for out-of-the-way convenience stores, pharmacies, and supermarkets that might have the magazine in stock. They quickly learned that bookstores were not worth their time; being more likely to carry comics, other collectors had beaten them to it. But they had mixed luck with the other merchants.

The hunt was both thrilling and maddening. They would enter a store nervously, walk directly to the magazine rack and case it for comic books. They would then carefully flip through displays to make sure they didn't overlook a *Thor* that had been sandwiched between or behind other titles. Most of the time, they searched in vain, as many stores carried only the popular titles, like Marvel's *Spiderman* and *Fantastic Four* and DC's *Batman* and *Superman*. Sometimes they would rejoice as they found a rare copy, only to discover that it had been rammed into the metal display carelessly by a merchant or a customer who didn't understand its value, causing damage to the spine or the cover, rendering it virtually worthless. More than once, a suspicious store clerk assumed they were trying to ogle some of the lewd adult magazines on display and threw them out of the store before they could complete their reconnaissance mission.

Yet, before the new year, they had managed to scrounge up a hoard of twenty-four additional near mint copies of *Thor* # 337. They split them evenly, each taking twelve, and duly bagged their investments to preserve them. All they had to do now was wait for the price to rise, although patience is not a commodity with which teenage boys are well endowed.

The first Friday of January 1984 was a chill, grey day with snow flurries, but the inclement weather failed to dampen Henry and Simon's spirits as they queued for the Bathurst streetcar. This would be the day when they learned how much their investment had appreciated. Henry sought distraction from the agony of waiting by playing "Which Would You Choose," their version of "Would You Rather."

"Alright, Simon, which would you choose: an A in next week's History exam or *Daredevil* 158?"

"The first Miller *Daredevil?*" Simon considered, "I'd have to go with that. I can always pick up my grade on the final."

"Good choice," his friend concurred. A very packed streetcar screeched to a halt in front on them. They clambered aboard and, unable to find seats, stood in back holding on to the metal pole.

"Okay," Henry continued, staring down at his shorter friend, "what about trip to the comic store or touching Debbie Bender's back?"

"Are you...? I mean.... Touching her back? Like what's your problem, asshole?" Simon exploded, his pimple-ridden face tinted dark red, as he peered around to see if anyone he knew had overheard. "Why would I want to touch her back? I'm not some weird stalker or pervert! I wouldn't mind hanging out with her or holding her hand. But touching her back? Who thinks of that? You're seriously messed up!"

"Geez! Sorry!" Henry backpedaled. "So what about the comic store or... holding Debbie Bender's hand?"

Once again, Simon glanced around quickly. While the middle-aged woman sitting down on the bench attached to the pole he was holding regarded them with a bemused smile, he was satisfied that no-one he knew was in earshot. "Sorry, pal, but definitely Debbie. Although I can do both, you know...."

The streetcar lurched forward suddenly, causing Simon to lose his balance and fall towards the middle-aged woman. He apologized, as Henry peppered him with another challenge. "Okay, then which would you choose: a date with Debbie Bender or *Amazing Fantasy #15?*"

Simon's azure eyes grew wide. "Get real, man! That's not even a fair choice! The *Amazing Fantasy*, of course!"

"That's the Simon I know," Henry said approvingly, pursing his lips. "Then what about Debbie Bender or *Spiderman* 122?"

"Where Green Goblin dies? That's a tough one.... Hey, this is our stop! We need to get off!"

He was saved from having to choose by the need to elbow his way through commuters to the rear exit doors. By the time they emerged on Queen Street, Henry had lost interest in the game and they began to sprint most of the kilometre separating Bathurst St. and the Silver Snail. Upon arrival, they quickly learned that their prayers had been answered: proudly mounted on the side wall with other prized comics was the *Thor* issue with Simonson's masterful cover. On the upper right-hand corner of its protective bag was a round lime-green sticker with its current price: fifty-eight dollars. It was now worth about fifty times its original Canadian dollar purchase price! They had struck gold.

After selecting their purchases for the month, including five copies each of the next *Thor* issue, #338, they gathered more intelligence from the managers at both Silver Snail and Dragon Lady, who both felt that the sky was the limit for #337. The manager at Dragon Lady expected that by their next visit in February it could be worth a hundred dollars. The boys were ecstatic.

On the way home, they debated what to do with their cache of gold. Henry entertained the idea of returning the next Monday afternoon after school and trading in ten of his *Thors* to lock in his gains. While the store would only buy back the comic for about seventy-five percent of its current value, he would probably get about ninety percent in a trade-in, which would yield him almost five hundred dollars to spend on coveted – and usually out-of-reach – wall comics. But Simon was loath to act precipitously. His heart was set on his white whale, his Moses on the summit of Mount Sinai, the copy of *Amazing Fantasy* #15 that graced Dragon Lady's wall. That required greater patience. If they waited another month, until it surpassed one hundred dollars, he would be able to trade his entire stash in for almost the price of the first ever appearance of Spiderman. The rest he would be able to fill in with savings from his babysitting and paper route earnings. Although Henry was wavering, he ultimately deferred to his friend's council and agreed to sit on his hoard for another month, awaiting even greater gains.

That night, however, Simon was troubled. *Was it really right to treat comics this way?* he wondered. He stared at a copy of the Simonson *Thor*. It *was* a beautiful cover. But he had found the story uninspiring and uninteresting. Why did he have sixteen copies of this dud, whereas his most treasured comics, his *Amazing Spidermans*, he had only one of? Did that make sense? Just because some nameless, faceless people found it desirable?

His mother noticed his consternation and asked him about it after dinner.

"Aw, it's nothing. You wouldn't understand," he evaded. "It's about comics."

"Try me," she insisted gently.

"Well, Henry and I bought lots of a special comic because it's gonna be huge and worth lots of money. Once that happens, I want to trade them in for an awesome one. It just... It just doesn't feel right, Mom." He glanced at her face and thought he read a bemused disinterest. "Aw, forget it. I said you wouldn't get it."

"No, I think I *do*, dear," his mother said. "There's much more to life than money, but I think you already know that or you wouldn't be asking me about this. I love the fact that you collect comics as works of art. I don't understand them myself, but it's clear that you appreciate them like I value an exquisite painting or a fine wine. You can treat them as a commodity. There's nothing wrong with it. But be careful. Because you may never again be able to see them for their beauty, which would be a terrible shame."

"I don't know. I'm doing it for the greatest work of comic art ever," Simon reasoned.

"Well, you'll figure it out, dear. You've got a good head on your shoulders. Just follow your conscience. It'll never lead you astray."

Typical mom advice, he thought. She means well, but she just doesn't get it.

In the end, the boys persevered, with great difficulty, until the first Friday in February. That day, they each brought their entire holdings of *Thor* #337 to school, carefully packed, so that they could trade them in downtown at the current price. But what would that be? Did it shoot past one hundred dollars? Henry was certain of it, although Simon sagely opined, without any clear basis, that seventy-five to one hundred was more likely.

Their excitement was so great that they couldn't concentrate on their classes. Notably, when Debbie Bender approached Simon immediately after French class at the end of the day, he quickly excused himself – "Sorry, Debbie. I gotta go" – and raced to his locker.

On the southbound streetcar, they were too anxious to talk. Instead, they each privately agonized about the likely price and whether they should trade their stashes if it had not yet reached one hundred dollars. It occurred to Henry that he was carrying over fifteen hundred dollars worth of merchandise, which caused him to tighten his grip on his knapsack and eye his fellow passengers warily. As they approached their stop, Simon suggested that they alter their routine and head directly to Dragon Lady, since he would need to trade in his *Thors* there to secure his holy grail, which at long last was within his grasp. Henry agreed. When they descended at Queen Street, Henry inhaled deeply and uttered, "This is it, man!" Simon nodded.

This time they trudged the distance to Dragon Lady slowly and carefully, rather than running, since they were afraid of damaging the precious cargo carefully packaged and insulated within their knapsacks. By the time they arrived, they were breathless with anticipation. Henry's hand trembled as he pulled open the door. Once inside, they searched in vain for Simonson's *Thor* on the wall behind the cash register, with all the other trophies.

"Must've sold out," Henry surmised, biting his chapped lower lip. Simon nodded, as his eyes rapaciously took notice of the *Amazing Fantasy* #15 that would shortly be his – a hunter studying his prey.

The manager was serving other customers, so they waved to him and continued to the back issue bins while they waited to talk to him. Simon gravitated to the *Amazing Spiderman* bins, while Henry drifted toward the *X-Men* title. On the way, Henry casually flipped through the most recent *Thor* back issues, just to pass the time. Suddenly he froze, his face turning ashen, the life force draining from his cheeks.

"Simon!" It was more an urgent, hoarse whisper than a cry.

Simon's attention was riveted on a copy of *Spiderman* #121 – the death of Gwen Stacy – in only fair condition for eleven dollars. Although the price was right, he was considering whether there was any point in purchasing it with such a badly water-damaged cover.

"Yeah, what?" he asked impatiently without turning his head.

"Look!" his friend implored him, still unable to raise his gravelly voice above a whisper.

Reluctantly, Simon put the comic he was holding back in its spot and turned to join his friend at the *Thor* bin. What he saw stopped him dead in his tracks. At the tail of the stock of *Thor* back issues were about fifteen to twenty copies of Simonson's *Thor* #337, with its ground-breaking cover, each labelled to sell for only twelve dollars and fifty cents!

"Whaa? How… how can that be?" Simon spat out inarticulately, as a sinking feeling commandeered the pit of his stomach. He felt weak, queasy.

"Makes no sense," Henry muttered despondently.

They positioned themselves near the cash and waited for the manager to finish his conversation with a middle-aged customer about the upcoming Marvel *Secret Wars* series.

"Hi guys!" he said pleasantly once he was free. "How are you both doing?"

Henry dispensed with the pleasantries. "What happened to *Thor*?" he barked.

"Oh, you haven't heard yet?" He saw from their faces that they hadn't. "The distributor pulled a fast one on us. They apparently held back many more copies of #337 than they had initially distributed, and then about three weeks ago, when the price was high, they flooded the market with their reserves."

"What? But why would they do that?" Simon asked.

"To make money." The manager smiled wryly. "I guess they saw what happened with the first Miller *Daredevil* and decided to cash in on Simonson's first *Thor* by controlling the game. In my view, it's pretty low."

"But... But you *told* us to buy them! We bought *tons* of them!" Henry charged.

"I know. I'm sorry. I also bought a bunch. I really thought it was a great opportunity," the manager declared solemnly, the cleft in his chin deepening.

"Well, can we at least trade in what we've bought?" Simon inquired. "We've got about thirty copies between us."

The manager shook his head. "I'm sorry. *Really* sorry. But we've got more than we need at this point. The owner won't let me buy any more. You're not the first customers to ask."

"So... what do we *do* with 'em all?" Henry demanded indignantly.

"I'm afraid there's not much you *can* do. You could try to sell them privately or at a comic convention. But the market's so flooded with them now that I don't think you'll get many takers.

You're probably best off holding on to them for now and hoping that, after a few years, the market for them improves a bit."

The boys were stunned into silence. There was nothing more to say or do, so they took leave of the store and headed back home dumbfounded, crestfallen, betrayed. As he left his temple, Simon stole a forlorn glance at the precious relic on the wall, which he knew now would never be his.

Later that evening, as he unpacked his knapsack in his room, Simon was fuming. "How *could* they?" he muttered aloud, clenching and unclenching his bony fists in anger. He tossed the *Thors* contemptuously on his dresser. He now was stuck with sixteen copies of a comic that, aside from the cover art, he did not enjoy, did not want. Which was virtually worthless. All because some greedy businesspeople conned him – conned everybody – to make some more money. Why would they do that to something as beautiful and magical – at the time he wouldn't have used the word "holy," but years later he would – as comics? Why would they debase them?

It seemed to him that the creature in Thor's armour on the cover was mocking him, that his war hammer was destroying not only the tranquility of the cover and the masthead, but also Simon's dreams, the joy he derived from collecting comics. He picked up the stack of comics and shoved them into the back of one his cardboard comic boxes. Then he scornfully kicked the box to the back of his closet.

On the first Friday of the following month, Henry was waiting at Simon's locker at the end of the school day, studying his sparse, almost translucent, teenage moustache in the small mirror. "You're late again!" he jeered when his friend finally arrived, accompanied by Debbie Bender.

"Oh, right," Simon said with obvious discomfort. "Sorry, man, but you go without me today. I'm gonna walk home with Debbie."

"Are you serious? It's the first Friday of the month!" Henry said incredulously.

"I know. I'm sorry.... Maybe next month."

Crestfallen, Henry mumbled, "Okay, I guess.... It's up to you, man. See ya, loser."

As Henry ambled off to the streetcar stop shaking his head, Debbie asked Simon, "Don't you want to go with Henry, like you always do? I don't mind."

Simon hesitated for a few seconds, then tentatively, hopefully, reached for her hand, which she bestowed upon him freely. "Nah," he said. "It's just a bunch of stupid comics."

The Rebellion

You might say that Jill held all the power in her marriage. Her husband, David, was blissfully mesmerized by her and would do anything to please her, a state of affairs that Jill employed all her coquetry to achieve and maintain. In ten years of marriage, not once did they fight. Instead, she would tell David what she wanted and then with a look, a smile, a caress, would melt any opposition from him.

Her reign over him was supreme. She would often wake him after midnight if she couldn't sleep and desired company or needed some warmth on a cold night. He would never disturb her slumber. He was forbidden to enter the bathroom while she was inside without knocking to request permission. It was her right and privilege, however, to come and go as she wished, without bothering to knock. Nor was her mastery simply a private affair. She had the authority to coax him into submission even if friends or family were present and did so if that was her whim. He never complained.

Nevertheless, she was anything but a cruel tyrant. She never threatened him or raised her voice. On the rare occasions when she believed David would be truly unhappy – which happened rarely – she would always graciously concede. More frequently, however, she would reward him handsomely for his sacrifices, liberally sharing all the riches of her treasury: her captivating smile, her heartfelt praise, other, more tangible, rewards.

Jill was always kind and sensitive to his needs. The first time she dragged him to the ballet – for him an immense sacrifice – she bade him to distract himself by imagining his recompense on their return home. During the performance, when his disenchantment was particularly palpable, she leaned over, brushing her chestnut locks against his cheek, and explained in a whisper exactly what that would be, her well-manicured hand resting carelessly on his lap. He appeared to watch the rest of the performance with great enthusiasm and excitement.

At times she exercised her power just to make sure that his planet remained steadfastly in orbit around her sun. One evening, for instance, he was ensconced upon the couch in the den, too engrossed in his book for her taste, while their young son assembled castles with his blocks on the black and gold geometric carpet. "Oh, there you are. After the day I had, I could really use one of your patented foot massages!" she declared.

"Sure, Sweets. I just want to finish this chapter first."

Ignoring him, she reclined with her head on the opposite armrest of the couch, thrusting her long, lithe legs into his lap, gently but firmly kicking away his book with one foot, pawing his thigh artfully with the other. He relented immediately with an impish grin. Dropping the book without even inserting the bookmark, he gingerly grabbed a foot, removed her ankle sock and began kneading her toes with his palm.

"Ahhh!" she purred contentedly, "*That's* what I needed." She wriggled her slender foot free of his grasp and pressed her toes tenderly to his mouth for him to kiss, satisfied that his focus was restored to the proper target.

Sometimes she teased him about it, as their little joke. One morning as they prepared for their commutes, she barged in on him after his shower, as he was drying himself. With a mischievous glance, she said, "David, would you be a dear and pick Ben-Ben up from daycare for me this afternoon?"

"Oh sorry, Sweets, but I can't.... I have a meeting then," he replied, always a little off balance when she wanted something.

She advanced toward him, a tiger on the prowl, and ran her hand along his inner thigh, underneath his towel. Leaning toward him, she whispered seductively in his ear, "Oh, that's too bad. I really wanted to have coffee with Amrita after work today... Are you *sure* you can't help me out?" She nibbled on his earlobe, blew on it softly, sending shivers of delight down his spine.

"I... I don't know," he protested without conviction, "It's an important meeting...."

Jill pulled his towel away, letting it drop carelessly to the floor, and began kissing his chest, his stomach. It was only a matter of time before he capitulated.

"I guess I could try to reschedule it...." he backtracked.

Her smile was naughty and triumphant, as it always was when he relented. "That's a sweet boy," she cooed, threading her fingers possessively through the curly black forest on his chest. "Now what do I like you to say to me when I let you help me out?" She unbuttoned her oversized pajama top, but held both loose flaps in place expectantly, fixing David's cobalt eyes with her own soft caramel toffee orbs.

Feverishly, he blurted out, "Thank you!" knowing that was what she wanted, to tease him, to make him acknowledge that he wasn't really inconvenienced, that it was all a game, that she wasn't mean.

She tossed away her top, revealing the contrast of her pert, pink breasts hovering above the crescent of her darker, silky stomach and poised provocatively to remove her pajama pants, as well, stopping again to say with a coy glance, "Thank you, what?"

"Thank you, my beautiful goddess!"

Her triumph complete, she threw off her pajama bottoms and pushed him back into the shower. They were both late for work that morning.

At the Second Cup that late spring afternoon, her conversation with Amrita revolved around her relationship with David, as it invariably did. Since their undergraduate years at York, where they had met in a first-year History lecture, their close friendship had endured their fiery competition, of late fuelled by their different approaches to life and relationships. Although Amrita was a modern feminist woman, she stemmed from a traditional Hindu family and retained many conventional practices and attitudes, including in her relationship with her husband Bob. She was thus a fascinating, paradoxical mix of old and new values. Jill, in contrast, was thoroughly modern.

"It's not natural to treat your husband like that, Jill. Face it, you're an abusive woman," Amrita accused, her velvety accent a cross between British and South Asian.

"That's ridiculous!" Jill pulled a sour face.

"Oh, come on! You have him wrapped around your little finger. You could order him to stand naked in the middle of Yonge Street and he would do it." The man at the next table glanced up from his laptop computer with interest.

"Yes, I suppose," Jill conceded with a giggle. "But it's not like that! I would never do something like that to him. I love him dearly!"

"That's right. You're Mother Theresa!" Amrita chortled, her voice dripping with irony. She brushed a pastry crumb off her navy cargo shorts.

"I don't *hurt* him; I make him happy. All day at work, he dreams of coming home and pleasing me. And you know what, I dream of pleasing him, too. After ten wonderful years of marriage, our relationship is still electric. Not many couples can say that," Jill proclaimed with a righteous edge to her voice.

"But you never let him do what he wants to do. Always dragging him to the ballet, the opera, shopping for dresses." Amrita let the accusations fly. "You never let him be a man! You won't ever let him spend his nights getting drunk with the boys and playing poker like Bob does. Or going to the ball game. And he's too afraid of you to stand up for himself."

"You don't understand at all! I don't tell him what he *can* do and what he *can't* do. And he's not *afraid* of me. Far from it! You know, Macchiavelli was wrong. It's far better to be *loved* than feared. I tell David what *I'd* like and then I get *him* to want that too. And, when I've worked my magic, he truly *does* want it. So in the end, he gets exactly what he wants."

"That's so self-serving and craven," Amrita barked, stifling a laugh.

"Admit it, Amrita. You're a little jealous."

"I'm not a *little* jealous. I'm *insanely* jealous! I'd love it if Bob were to do what I wanted to do more. But it's mean what you do. It's wrong!" Amrita took a sip of her latte, as if to punctuate her charge.

"What's so wrong? I give him what *he* wants, too. You've got to realize that men aren't very complicated. They want to be touched. To feel useful. To be loved. To be praised. And, yes, they want sex. If you give them what they want with a smile on your face, they'll do absolutely *anything* for you."

"But it's so anti-feminist to have to cater to your man's sexual desires." Amrita glared at the man at the neighbouring table with her dark, almost ebony, eyes, scaring him back into his cappuccino, which he studied with exaggerated interest.

"I completely disagree! There's nothing more *feminist* than what I do. I don't use sex as a *weapon*, in a coercive or dominating way. I never threaten to *punish* him if he doesn't do what I want. Instead, I *nurture* him, make him see that it's better for *both* of us if he cooperates." Jill, leaned forward, her elbows on the table, growing more animated and intense. "Don't look at me like that. Instead of a *competition*, where we want different things and only one of us can get our way, I create *harmony*, where we both want the same thing – what *I* want – so there is no conflict."

"My mistake. You're not Mother Theresa; you're Gloria Steinem!"

"Amrita, I am such a feminist that I really believe that if women ruled the world like I rule my household, if there was a matriarchy instead of a patriarchy, there'd never be conflict – at least not involving men. Between women there'd still be plenty.

And don't make the mistake of thinking I do *anything* I don't enjoy. Men aren't the *only* ones who enjoy sex!" The man at the next table coughed audibly. Jill smiled at him warmly, while Amrita assaulted him with another angry look.

"All I can say is that it's cruel to treat him like that, to control him," Amrita sputtered, pursing her lips, tapping her cardboard cup on the table.

"I doubt *he'd* say that. I'm sure he wouldn't have it any other way. The key is: I take *generously*. If I took everything he gave me without a smile, without rewarding him, that would be cruel. Nasty even. Instead of ignoring him or scowling at him like other wives do to their husbands, making them feel unloved, all alone, I always let David know exactly how much I appreciate him. So while I make him do every little thing I want... *every* little thing... he feels like a king," Jill crowed, rubbing her slender fingers together to illustrate her mastery.

Amrita smirked suddenly, remembering a barb she had prepared for this afternoon. "Jack went up the hill for Jill, to fetch a pail of water. Jack fell down and broke his crown, while Jill just roared with laughter!"

"Very funny!" Jill declared drily. "You know, I'd rather control him lovingly than have him control me, like men tend to do – like Bob does to *you* – by yelling and threatening." Amrita coloured. "But there's really nothing mean about it..."

"Not at all!" Amrita interrupted scornfully. "You know, Jill, I still can't decide if you're a nasty bitch or just a whore!"

"Oh, please! I give myself only when *I* want. The long and the short of it is, though, that I am so in love with him," Jill continued earnestly, as Amrita raised her eyebrows. "He's the sweetest man in the world. All he wants to do is please me. And

I please him by letting him do what *I* want. And I thank him for it, *reward* him for it. I think we have a model marriage, that we are the happiest couple in the world!"

Not that David would have put it exactly that way. In truth, he didn't really have many complaints, although he felt a bit sheepish and controlled when he viewed himself through other people's eyes. Since they loved each other and he was more than content with his marriage, he decided it wasn't worth fighting over. It was something he could easily live with, if it didn't embarrass him with the outside world. Other people, however, were only too eager to hold a mirror up to him, to criticize him. One such conversation with his friend Kevin after they played squash the following week helped nurture the sense of shame in him.

"So can you come over for Poker on Saturday evening?" Kevin asked, as he towelled himself off in the locker room, his short hairy arms like windshield wipers, sweeping the white towel across his stout, bushy legs in fluid motions.

David reddened. "Uh, I'd love to, Kevin. But Jill got us tickets for the Four Seasons Centre. There's an opera she really wants to see. I'll come another time."

"You *hate* opera! Like, you need to stand up for yourself more, dude!" Kevin punched David's shoulder lightly to add emphasis.

"Aw, it's not like that. I just promised her I'd go when this show came to town," David responded uncomfortably. He tried to change the subject while fiddling with the silver and black combination lock on his locker. "Hey, did you catch last night's game? Kessel finally broke out of his slump. If he were to spread his scoring out, they'd be unstoppable."

"Forget Kessel, dude. You're the one whose got problems," Kevin pressed, as he pulled out a comb and struggled with his curly red mane.

"Really, Kev. It's no big deal. I don't mind going to the opera."

"Look, I don't want to butt into your marriage," Kevin asserted, "but we've been friends for ages, and I really think you need help. Jill's a nice girl, but__"

"Woman," David corrected, wrinkling his fleshy nose. He tossed his towel on the floor and began pulling on his clothing, glancing around furtively.

"Fine, she a nice *woman*," Kevin conceded, "but she's too controlling. She's got you whipped! You need to stand up to her! Be a man!"

David was annoyed, principally because nothing his friend was saying was far from the mark, at least from an outside observer's perspective. But he also didn't like talking about private matters in such a public setting. "You can't understand someone else's marriage from the outside. Everyone negotiates their own unique bargain, which is right for them. It might look stupid to other people, but if it works for us, that's all that matters." He flung his running shoes onto the bottom shelf a little too aggressively and grabbed his brown loafers.

"Does it work for *you*, or just for *her*?"

It took a while for David to reply. "For both of us," he said at last, eager to end the discussion.

"Are you sure? Like, what does she ever do for you?"

David blushed, his red cheeks a stunning contrast to his thinning black hair, his blue-green eyes. "She keeps me happy."

"Really? Well, how often do you... ah, *you* know?" asked Kevin intrusively.

"I don't know.... Maybe four or five times a week."

"Four or five times a *week*! Wow!" Kevin's grey eyes widened.

"Sometimes more, sometimes less. It really depends," David qualified apologetically.

Kevin was silent, mulling that over as he packed his racquet and exercise clothing moodily into his canvas sports bag.

"What about you and Karen?" David asked.

"Nowhere near that!" Kevin snapped. "Four or five times a week! That's not even *human*!"

"Sorry, Kev. I didn't mean to intrude."

"But that's really not the point, dude," Kevin decided, recovering the thrust of his argument. "You'd have just as much sex if you stood your ground, you know. Women actually like a strong-willed man. Jill would have more respect for you if you fought for what you wanted."

"Well, I uh…" mumbled David, frustrated that he'd never be able to explain to his friends or family the beauty of his marriage, the miraculous love he shared with Jill. They couldn't get past what they viewed as abusive and unnatural. "Listen, I love Jill. Our marriage is based on love, not power…"

"Of course, dude," Kevin interrupted, as they ambled toward the gym's exit. "I'm not suggesting otherwise. But you can still assert yourself more and make sure she doesn't walk all over you."

"Yeah, I suppose you're right…" David conceded awkwardly, as he pushed through the door and approached the parking lot.

It all came crashing down one summer, when Jill's brother came for an extended visit with his family. David found his loud, overbearing, insensitive brother-in-law intolerable. In truth, he was difficult for Jill to stomach, too. But he was blood, and she was determined to behave properly. When he called to announce that his family would be visiting Toronto from out west for two weeks and wanted to stay with David and Jill in their Forest Hill home, she understood it would be immensely trying, but knew that they had to consent graciously. David strongly objected to such a lengthy stay, but Jill surmounted his opposition with her usual deftness.

From the outset, Jill's brother was patronizing and insulting. Jill and David had prepared a lavish welcome meal for their guests, only to be criticized, to have their deeply-held values ridiculed.

"Is that all you're serving us? Grass and beans?" her brother chided mockingly. For moral reasons, David and Jill had become vegetarians, a choice Jill's brother did not respect.

"It's hardly grass and beans, Alex. General Tso's mock chicken, Thai red curry tofu and spring rolls. It's like a restaurant meal," Jill answered, eyeing David warily and hoping to avert a major confrontation.

"If there's no meat, it's not any restaurant *I'd* go to," retorted Alex. Though their personalities differed, he and Jill bore a strong sibling resemblance, with caramel toffee eyes, oblong faces, and distinguished, angular noses. The similarity always grated on David.

Trying to be conciliatory, Alex's wife condescended, "*Well*, the General Tso is actually quite good. For vegetarian food, anyway."

David hated it when Jill's family trivialized their values, but especially when they did so in front of their young son. His face reddening, he snapped, "If you don't like what we eat, you're more than welcome to go elsewhere for your meals."

"Oh, but we came to see *you*," Alex rejoined. "I suppose we can tolerate *this* stuff to eat together as a family. But have you ever sunk your teeth into a good sirloin steak, Davy? No way you could remain a vegetarian after that."

"As you very well know, I wasn't a vegetarian all my life. I've had plenty of steaks. But we decided to give that up for the planet. And because it's cruel to animals." David hated when Alex called him Davy.

"I'm not sure you three eat enough to really help the planet much. And if you're worried about cruelty, you really shouldn't eat plants either. Why are you so willing to massacre innocent plants? They're living things too! And what about all the bacteria in water that you kill when you take a drink?" Alex mocked him.

Seeing David's blood pressure rising by the minute, Jill threw him an imploring look, while sliding her foot up his thigh under the table. David responded with an angry scowl – a warning sign if Jill had ever seen one. He then excused himself from the table to put Ben to bed.

Later that night, David and Jill took refuge in their bedroom, preparing to sleep. David chewed on a pink antacid tablet to neutralize the acid bubbling up into his throat.

"What an obnoxious ass!" he sputtered, belching slightly to relieve the burning sensation.

"You're right, Babe. I'm sorry he's like that. Mom and Dad never disciplined him. They turned him into a self-centred terror." She tried to soothe him by rubbing his back gently with her small, round hands.

"How did *you* turn out okay?" he asked.

"Well, aside from being perfect?" she teased. "I guess they realized that they'd spoiled Alex badly, so they took parenting more seriously with me."

"It's going to be difficult for me to tolerate them for *two weeks*."

"I know, Baby. I really, *really*, appreciate this." She started kissing his shoulders, biting them gently, running her fingers behind his ears. She shut the lights and they settled onto the bed. Just then, the air was pierced by the shrill sound of a brass horn.

David lunged at the light switch. "Is that…" he uttered, in shock.

"I think he's playing his *trumpet*!" Jill exclaimed in disbelief.

Ben came scampering into their room. "What's dat noise, Mommy?" he asked, rubbing the sleep from his eyes.

"Don't worry, Ben-Ben," she replied. "It's just Uncle Alex playing his trumpet. I know it's late. I'll ask him to stop."

Before she could take care of it, David girded himself in his robe, the grey terry belt dangling clumsily, and galloped down the stairs of their Georgian revival-style house to the guest-suite in the basement.

"Just *what* do you think you're doing? It's eleven o'clock and everybody's in bed!" David roared.

"Oh, sorry 'bout that, Davy. I like to relax at night by playing a bit," Alex said matter-of-factly, removing the brass instrument from his lips.

"What is *wrong* with you? You're not in your own home, you know. Show some consideration for someone other than *your-self*!" David shouted, shaking with rage.

"You don't have to get so uppity. Geez, I get it! You're not a music lover. I won't play while you're around again," Alex snapped with indignation. Turning his attention to his daughters, he continued, "Sorry girls. Uncle Davy doesn't want me to play you a goodnight song."

"My name is David, you inconsiderate lout!"

At that moment, Jill arrived after settling Ben back to bed. She pulled David aside and told him to go back upstairs, while she had a heated discussion with Alex about ground rules for his visit. Reluctantly, he consented.

When she returned to their bedroom, David was pacing back-and-forth, his stomach on fire. "I want him gone, Jill!" He didn't ordinarily use her name, except in formal settings.

"He's really annoying and inconsiderate, Babe, but he's my only brother. What can I do?" she asked rhetorically. She reached for his arm, but he shook her off brusquely.

"I don't *care*! He's got to go! I can't *take* him!"

Ordinarily, on the rare occasions when he was adamant, she would give way. But she just couldn't evict her own brother, could she? She began to work David. "I know, Babe. But please *try*, for *me*," she said, as she launched an all-out assault on his citadels – his ears, his neck, his thighs, elsewhere.

She felt him resisting, which was both unprecedented and alarming. Undeterred, she escalated to her nuclear option: she nibbled on his neck, which always overcame all resistance, reducing him to putty in her hands. It didn't fail her.

"Well," he murmured, relenting, "you're going to have to keep him away from me and make sure he follows our rules while he's in the house."

"You're so good to me, Babe. And I'm *so* grateful," Jill breathed, as she switched off the light and continued kissing him.

The next crisis occurred the following morning, as they were getting ready for work. As Jill, David and Ben descended for breakfast, they were assaulted by the acrid odour of cigarette smoke on the stairs.

"He wouldn't *dare*. Would he?" David asked in horror. Jill just grimaced, no doubt fearing that he might.

When they reached the kitchen, Alex was reclining on David's chair, puffing away on a lit cigarette. "Morning, sis!" he called majestically.

"Alex, please put that out!" Jill commanded. "We don't smoke in this house."

"Take it easy, Jill," Alex bristled. "I don't smoke at home – Meghan won't let me. She can't stand the smoke. Says its unhealthy for the girls. She *does* let smoke when I'm on vacation, though. That's why I'm doing it here."

"So you don't want to stink up your house or get your kids sick, but it's okay to do it to *our* home and *our* son?" David roared indignantly.

"If you want to smoke outside on the porch, that's fine. But don't do it inside *again*," Jill intervened sternly.

Alex complied, muttering "I don't see what the big deal is…" as he exited to the porch.

Jill quickly swept up the cigarette butts that had been left on the kitchen table, wrenched open the window over the kitchen sink and proceeded to prepare Ben's breakfast. David was breathing heavily – fiery, sonorous, nasal breaths – but afraid of being late for work he let the incident pass without further comment for the time being. For the second time since Alex arrived, though, he flashed Jill a violent look.

Over the next two days, their guests' assault on their formerly tranquil home intensified. David endured insulting comments about his profession – "I can't imagine anything more *boring* than being a chartered accountant" – and his mother – "Hey, Ben-Ben! Look at this picture of your Nana from Mommy and Daddy's wedding. Doesn't she look like Miss Piggy in that dress?" He was incensed when Meghan showed Ben pictures of their winter vacation in California, including one in which she lounged topless on a clothing-optional beach – "Oh, come on! Didn't Jill breastfeed him?" Their guests frequently used foul language in front of Ben – "This isn't the 1950s, Davy! Everybody says that nowadays." Their completely undisciplined daughters had a food fight in their hosts' living room, spraying peanut butter on their original Steven Shearer painting – "I think it's wonderful that they feel so comfortable in your home, don't you Davy?" Through it all, David exhibited superhuman restraint for Jill's sake, though his stomach churned like a washing machine on the spin cycle. For her part, Jill thanked him liberally in her own special manner, all the while trying unsuccessfully to curb her brother's most egregious transgressions.

Despite her best efforts, however, the breaking point came on the fourth evening of their sojourn, when Alex and Meghan collected Ben from daycare so that their hosts could enjoy a night out. Jill and David had bought tickets for a play at the Mirvish Theater, but Jill had accidentally forgotten them on her night table at home, necessitating a quick jaunt home before dinner. As they walked in on their unsuspecting guests, they found them greedily consuming McDonald's quarter pounders on their kitchen table, with paper bags and plastic cutlery scattered across the terra cotta floor. What's more, their own vegetarian son, who had never eaten meat in his lifetime, was sprawled across the floor munching on his own hamburger!

"How... how *dare* you?" David spat out, shaking in his fury.

"Oh, we didn't expect you. You weren't supposed to see that," Alex conceded.

"You mean you were going to feed Ben-Ben meat, against our wishes, without even telling us? What is *wrong* with you, Alex?" Jill chimed in.

"It's no big deal, Jill. He could use the protein, you know," Alex asserted.

"Aaaaarrrgghhh!!!!!" Their monstrous, self-centred insensitivity reduced David to an inarticulate paroxysm of rage, his face flushed crimson, his vision blurring, a sharp pain enveloping his chest and stomach.

Unaccustomed to seeing his parents so angry and fearing that he may have been responsible, Ben burst into tears and started bawling uncontrollably. Jill smothered him in her arms, stroking his hair, assuring him, "It's okay, baby." Then, concerned about David, she implored him, "I'll take care of this, David. Why don't you go outside and calm down a bit?"

Too enraged to speak, David acquiesced. He exited the house and circled the block multiple times. He kept repeating, "How *dare* they? Who do they think they *are*?" under his breath, but audibly enough for one of his neighbours to stare at him in bemusement. He began to wonder how Jill could keep enabling her brother, letting him get away with murder. Then he remembered Kevin admonishing him to assert himself.

When he returned half an hour later, he encountered Alex in the hallway. "Listen, Davy, I didn't want to__" his brother-in-law began.

"I don't want to *hear* it," David cut him off. "Where's Jill?"

"She went to put Ben-Ben to bed."

David shoved him aside and bounded up the stairs. Ben was already asleep, so he searched for Jill in the master bedroom. Hearing him enter, Jill called out, "I'm in the loo, Babe. I'll be out in a few minutes."

David inhaled deeply and burst into the bathroom, finding his wife astride her porcelain throne.

"Hey! *I'm* in here! Please stay out and I'll join you soon." She was shocked to have her privacy invaded and more than a little embarrassed to be surprised in this delicate position.

"I'm not waiting, Jill. I want your brother out *now*!" David said sternly.

"Hey... I know you're upset, Babe. I am, too. But he's my only brother. It's only another__"

"I *know* he's your brother, but let's face it. He's an inconsiderate, insensitive *pig*! I'm not gonna put up with him for another minute. I want him gone *tonight*!" He cut in resolutely.

"Listen, Baby..." she began softly, as she got up awkwardly from the toilet to approach him.

"No! Don't 'Baby' me! I'm *serious*. He has to *go*!" David barked.

Jill was at a loss. Wounded. How could he talk to her this way? Sure, he was right. Alex *was* a pig. But why wouldn't he let her calm him down and find a reasonable solution? She needed to restore the natural order. She reached over to stroke his arm, but he withdrew it aggressively.

"Don't touch me! Don't try to manipulate me! Either *you* send him packing or *I* will. Those are your choices," David warned, feeling more confident, more empowered, by the minute.

David's words, his defiance, cut Jill to the core. *Manipulate* him! Yes, she supposed she did manipulate him, but it wasn't quite like *that*, was it? Had Amrita been correct after all? With tears in her eyes and an expression of shock, remorse, defeat, Jill nodded sadly and submitted. "I'll tell him."

As she washed her hands and vacated the bathroom in turmoil, David was strangely exultant. He had stood up to her and emerged victorious, toppled her from her imperial perch. *She* was bending to *his* will. This was his declaration of independence. He would no longer be pushed around, a non-entity.

On a dreary, rainy Friday afternoon several years later, Jill lingered in the living room of the same Forest Hill home, scrutinizing their wedding photograph in its gilded silver frame. How happy they had looked! David – tall, short-haired, muscular David, in the black tuxedo with the matching bowtie that he had disliked intensely, but graciously wore to indulge his bride – positively beamed. And she, in her wedding finery, also tall, but still a head shorter, sporting the glint in her eyes that she always had when she got exactly what she wanted. The sheen of victory. Jill sighed deeply.

Looking up at the staircase through the living room archway, she called, "C'mon guys! You're gonna be late!" Amid the tumult of footfalls, she received her reply, "Coming, Ma!"

Her gaze returned to the photograph, which she still displayed, despite everything. How had they been derailed? Was it really just Alex's visit? Or had it been something deeper? Certainly, she reflected, her eyes glistening, her brother's visit had begun the slide to oblivion. After that, their relationship was never the same again. It had lost its spark. They who had been inseparable slowly gravitated apart. Initially, their conversations grew cordial rather than intimate. They touched less. Eventually, their estrangement grew, a note of formality was introduced. David spent more time at work, more evenings with his friends doing the things guys did. Even when they were home together, they gravitated to their own separate corners of the house, pursuing their own individual aims, with Ben as their only common pursuit.

Her reverie was interrupted by the furious pounding on the ceiling above her, like an out-of-control paint mixer. "Hey," she cried, "don't run upstairs! The whole house is shaking!"

"Sorry," Ben yelled. "We're almost ready."

But how had she allowed that to happen? Why didn't she do something? She shook her head mournfully, her still-lustrous chestnut hair quivering ever so slightly. Oh, how she would have loved to restore the affectionate, nurturing matriarchy that David had upended, the heavenly manna that had fed their glorious marriage. But how could she? She had lost the means. The easy confidence that had once fueled her empire had abandoned her. Every time she desired to coax him into submission as she used to, she was utterly paralyzed by the prospect of failure – something that had been inconceivable before. What if he resisted, called her manipulative, mean? That would have been too much for her to bear. So she refrained, as they drifted further and further off course.

With the clatter of the rain against the window, she wondered whether David too might have welcomed a restoration. Once she had thrown Alex out, perhaps he would have gladly surrendered to her, allowed her to place her soft, loving yoke around his neck again. He certainly gave her no indication. But perhaps he, too, had become a prisoner of his newfound pride, the surly defiance that had been introduced into his formerly docile eyes. Perhaps, having stormed her Olympus, triumphed over her majesty, he could not easily return to the land of the mortals, however much he might have wished to. Perhaps....

In any event, the holiness of their union had passed, never to be reborn. They had been banished from the garden. Not even Lisa's birth that winter had been able to save them. When they divorced a few years later, their friends exchanged knowing glances, claiming that it had been inevitable. Jill had been too controlling, they opined, David too weak. But Jill wasn't so certain. She now wondered whether their sin had been to try to reconcile their too precious pearl, their wondrous nirvana, with the baseness of a mundane world. She caressed the photograph delicately with her forefinger.

An unholy rumble on the staircase signalled the arrival of Ben and Lisa, overnight bags in hand. "We're ready," Lisa announced through the gap where her front teeth used to be.

"Did you remember your toothbrushes? Your underwear?" Jill asked.

"Got 'em," Ben said. "I helped Lisa pack."

"Good job," his mother said, crossing into the hall to collect her purse, her keys.

"I can't wait to see Daddy," Ben said excitedly. "I really miss him."

"Me, too," Lisa, now five years old, with short black bangs and David's sparkling cobalt eyes, chimed in.

"Me, too," echoed Jill wistfully. "Me, too."

The Magic Saxophone

B rian's life did not work out as planned.
When he received his doctorate in anthropology from McGill, his heart was set on an academic career, hopefully as a professor at a prestigious university. Unfortunately, he hit the job market just when the 2008 economic crisis hit the world. With almost no universities hiring and a glut of candidates clamouring for positions, he was forced to give up on his dream of studying Central American indigenous tribes and consider other, more mundane, career options. Yet, in a bad economy, Ph.D.s in anthropology were not in high demand. So, after a fruitless two-year search for something that would satisfy him, necessity compelled him to settle for what he considered a dead-end office job in a small Montreal food distributing company, at the mercy of an abusive boss that was never satisfied with his efforts. Instead of the intellectually rewarding life of a university professor, the allure of field research, he had settled into a professional life of drudgery, with no hope of escape.

His home life had not fared much better. True, he had married for love and still was fond of his wife. But they had both hoped to have a large family, and their inability to have children had taken a heavy toll on their relationship. In the early years of their marriage, they dealt with the frustration of trying and failing while all their friends were growing their families. The pressure of their parents' expectations only compounded the disappointment.

Eventually, they overcame their embarrassment and sought professional help. After several unsuccessful IVF treatments in Montreal, with the support of the provincial health insurance plan, they decided to pay out-of-pocket for an exclusive American clinic in suburban New York. The only tangible results were a depleted bank account and more agonizing failure. The stress of each treatment – the testing, the cycles of ovarian suppression and stimulation, the egg retrieval and fertilization, the embryo transfer, the endless, gut-wrenching waiting between steps and between trials – the inevitable bitter disappointment, caused them to withdraw within themselves. They grew estranged from friends, both to escape embarrassing, probing questions and to avoid hearing the painful stories about their friends' children. Even their own families became more than they could bear, leading them to visit their parents and siblings with decreasing frequency.

By now, both in their mid-forties, they had resigned themselves to childlessness. His wife had been eager to consider adoption, but Brian refused, saying they were already too old. Moreover, he asked bitterly, who wants to raise someone else's child? His wife had reluctantly accepted his decision and invested herself more heavily in her career as an architect.

Over time, Brian had grown increasingly despondent and resentful of his wife for coming to terms with a life without children. Furthermore, her professional success, which used to be a source of pride for him, now roiled him, as it held a mirror up to his own failure. As his outlook turned darker, they began to quarrel more. He also drank more frequently in the evenings, "just to help him sleep," he assured his wife, although she noticed that he slept less since he started. The very fabric of their marriage was unravelling.

To take his mind off his failures and attempt to alleviate their growing estrangement, his wife insisted that they spend their Sundays antique-hunting in the countryside, like they used to early in their marriage. So it was that, on a crisp Sunday afternoon in mid-October, Brian and his wife pulled up outside Chiasson's Antiques, a quaint curio store in the Eastern Townships, near Sutton, QC.

Despite the glorious weather – fifteen degrees and not a cloud in the sky, a blanket of auburn and amber leaves crinkling underfoot – Brian was in a foul mood. "I don't know why we're wasting our time," he snapped testily as he climbed out of the car. "Shopping isn't going to solve anything. I'd rather just turn back."

His wife was embarrassed about him arguing in public, so she tried to soothe him without thinking, carelessly treading on his sensibilities. "It's just a mid-life crisis, Brian. You'll get past it,"

"Mid-life crisis, Heather! My whole *life* is a mid-life crisis!" he exploded. "I'm not having an affair or buying a sports car. I have *real* problems that simply *can't* be fixed!" Nothing enraged him more than when she trivialized his plight. She hadn't meant to, but it was difficult to be diplomatic all the time, to walk on eggshells, and she frequently said exactly the wrong thing when she was trying to be helpful. The truth was, though, that she set him off no matter what she said nowadays.

"I know you're hurting," she responded earnestly. "I'm not your enemy; I'm hurting, too. But it's no-one's fault and you can't fritter the rest of your life away just because we've been dealt a bad hand."

She reached for his arm to mollify him, but he yanked it brusquely away and burst into the shop. The proprietor, Monsieur Chiasson, welcomed him with a friendly, "Soyez le bienvenue, monsieur," but Brian just grunted and pushed past him. Heather followed Brian into the shop and smiled timidly but politely at the owner before gravitating to a cabinet displaying china dolls. Brian wandered through the musty aisles without actually seeing anything. In his head, he continued the argument with his wife, shaking his head once to emphasize a point he scored in his mind's eye.

In a dark corner of the shop, he absently rummaged through a motley collection of jazz records, when he noticed a large, black, rectangular wooden instrument case behind them. The wood was badly warped, but he felt an unexplainable urge to discover what was inside. Undoing the rusted clasps, he lifted the lid to reveal a black lacquered tenor saxophone with lustreless brass keys. The faded old instrument with scratches on its bell was singularly unimpressive, yet it captured his attention. Inexplicably, for he had never played an instrument before nor had he showed any inclination in that direction, he ran his stubby fingers along its body, stroking its keys almost lovingly.

"What do you have there?" asked Heather, who sidled up to join him, hoping that the storm had abated.

"A saxophone...." he replied thoughtfully, all traces of anger gone from his voice.

Heather looked closely at the instrument, wrinkling her Roman nose. It was clearly the worse for wear. She started to ask, "What would you do with...." but then checked herself, not wanting to say the wrong thing again. "I mean, do you think you'd want to learn how to play something like that?"

"No.... I don't think so...." he replied, his voice trailing.

The proprietor approached the couple, asking them, "Je peux vous aider?"

Brian started to say no, when Heather interrupted in French, "How much are you asking for this old saxophone?"

"This is a most curious instrument. I've had it in the store for many years. I bought it from a senile old widow, who swore that it was enchanted – a magic saxophone. Before she left it with me, she insisted that it must never be played in front of other people," the antique dealer ruminated. "In all the years I've had it, you're the first people who even noticed it. I think I bought it from her for $200 and, after all this time, I'd be willing to break even and charge you $200."

Again, Brian started muttering that he was just looking at it, when Heather, observing the change in her husband's mood since he saw the battered saxophone, cut in, "Oh, Brian, why not? It could be fun for you to learn to play."

"Do you think so?" he asked, with growing interest. "It's a lot of money to throw away."

"We can afford $200, Brian," his wife countered. She turned back to the shop owner and asked in French, "Can he try it out?"

"I'm sorry, Madame, but it's missing key accessories, including the mouthpiece," Chiasson replied.

"That's okay, monsieur," she reassured him. And then to Brian she pleaded, "Please buy it. It'd be great to have live music in the house."

"But I don't have time to take lessons. It doesn't seem reasonable," he said weakly.

"You could teach your*self*, with the Youtube videos that you're always using to learn how to do home repairs," she pressed.

"I suppose I could…." he assented weakly. That settled the matter. They paid the proprietor and left the store in possession of a ramshackle saxophone, or parts thereof. As they returned to the car, Heather, with an urge to capitalize on this welcome distraction, insisted that they return to Montreal immediately and visit the Archambault music store to equip the saxophone properly. All through the ride back, they talked with some excitement about the songs he wanted to learn.

At the Archambault store on Sainte-Catherine Street, they showed the saxophone to a salesclerk, who laughed good-naturedly.

"That's a discontinued Selmer and it's in pretty bad shape. See the scratches here? The small hole in the bell? The little dent in the neck? I'm not sure you'll be able to get a true sound out of it. You'd be better off buying a new one," he told them.

Brian thanked him for his advice, but said that he wanted to learn on his Selmer and then buy a new one later, if he took to the instrument. He just wanted to purchase what he needed to play it.

The clerk shrugged and said, "Okay, it's up to you, Monsieur. You're going to need a mouthpiece, a ligature, a box of reeds and a strap, to begin with."

"Good. How much will that cost?" Heather asked.

"Well, it depends what you want? Have you ever blown a sax before?" the clerk asked. Brian shook his head. The clerk grabbed a box of Vandoren 2-strength reeds. "These will be good to start with then. You can move to stronger reeds when you get used to the embouchure. What kind of music you want to play?"

Brian answered without hesitation, "Jazz, the blues, some rock."

The clerk pulled out a Yamaha 5C mouthpiece and paired it with a Rovner 2R ligature. "This should start you out and work well with a range of music styles. Once you get good and you want a distinct sound, we can move you up to a more tailored option."

He pulled out a basic sax strap, asking, "Anything else you need to go with this?"

Brian browsed the display of saxophone accessories with growing excitement and selected a cleaning cloth with a weighted string for drying out the body and an orange Reedjuvenate cylinder to preserve his reeds. He then looked at the clerk sheepishly, asking him for a beginner's book that could help him learn on his own.

"Monsieur, you'd truly be better off taking lessons. I could help set you up with someone," he advised.

"No, maybe later," Brian said, the scowl that perpetually inhabited his face nowadays somehow less pronounced.

In the end, they laid out more on accessories than they had spent on the instrument itself, but they left the store with something they had not enjoyed in quite a while: enthusiasm.

For the next few weeks, he threw himself into his music lessons at every spare moment. They transformed the small basement of their West Island bungalow into his music studio, equipped with a metal music stand and a small lacquered table to anchor the laptop computer and large external monitor which would serve as his teacher. In the first few days he learned how to read music notes. Soon, he learned the fingering for all the full notes between high C and low C and did mouth exercises to develop the proper embouchure. With the help of his beginner's book and online tutorials, by mid-November he taught himself to play simple children's songs and some elementary scales. His repertory included *London Bridge, Mary Had a Little Lamb, Au Claire de la Lune*, and other such basic melodies. Heather would ask him to play for her, but he refused, saying he wasn't good enough yet.

Each night after his music sessions, Brian would inevitably hit the bottle. If anything, he drank more heavily than before. Sometimes, in a drunken delirium he would stammer pitifully, clutching his saxophone tightly as if it were a life vest, peering intently at it as if addressing it, "B... but where did it go? Wh... why can't I find it?"

On one such occasion, Heather tried to soothe him, taking his hand, saying "What, Brian? What are you looking for? Can *I* help you?" Wrenching himself free, he whined, "You c... can't understand. Just leave me alone!"

Feeling hurt, abandoned, ashamed, she lashed back out at him with venom, "I can't keep doing this, Brian! Stop wallowing in self-pity and thinking only of yourself. You're *making* yourself a failure!" Her words stung Brian through his alcoholic haze. He fell back in his chair dazed, with a look of pain, of horror, a wounded deer at the side of the highway, murmuring "Can't find it...." while Heather went upstairs to cry herself to sleep.

Over time, Brian gained confidence in his abilities, amazed at the progress he had made in such a short time. By January, after only three months, he had learned to play advanced pieces that are too complex and technical for beginners: Clarence Clemens' solo from *Jungleland*, the solo from Pink Floyd's *Money*, with all its sharps, flats, and multiple *glissandos*. Delighted by his prowess, he invited Heather to his music room for a practice session. As she listened to the two-minute *Jungleland* solo he blew with the battered instrument, she couldn't contain her surprise. "Brian," she said, "that was truly unbelievable!" He beamed with pride, a sensation he had not experienced for many years.

From then on, he let Heather work downstairs whenever he practiced. Happy to be a part of his life again, at least in this small sphere, she would encourage him while she sat on their old futon editing interior plans she had brought home from the office. Brian was pleased to have an appreciative audience, and frequently asked for her feedback on his sound. She never failed to support him.

One cold winter night, after he practiced all night, his wife gently urged him to come to bed without drinking. He put up no resistance and went to the bathroom to prepare for bed. Inspecting himself in the bathroom mirror, with the howl of the bitter wind outside, chill air seeping through the poorly-insulated window, he noticed his badly-receding hairline, the deep ridges on his forehead, the eyes deadened by failure, the once-handsome face tarnished by time and too many disappointments. He sighed morosely. *All the promise I had in life has been wasted.* He slunk to the kitchen, muttering "What a waste! What a waste!" and gulped down half a bottle of whisky, remaining there all night.

At 3 AM, Heather found him sprawled over the old futon in their basement, his open saxophone case across his lap. He whispered incoherently to no-one in particular, "I... want to. I've wanted to for such... a long time. B... but the path is so-o-o hard to find...." She covered him with a blanket and went back to bed. As she climbed the basement stairs, she thought she heard him mumble, "S... sometimes it's hard to see... if you d... don't remember how to l... l... look."

As the winter progressed, Brian became more heavily invested in his saxophone. Playing music was all he could think about during the interminable days. It made the drudgery of his job more bearable. Although Brian's boss continued to ride him, it stopped bothering him because he focused on what really mattered: playing music at night. Often during the workday, while he performed a particularly monotonous task, he would play one of his pieces in his head, fingering the keys in his mind's eye.

Significantly, with the greater peace that his music bestowed upon him, he started drinking less. Some nights he didn't partake at all. More frequently, he would imbibe a little before bed, but not enough to get soused. Only rarely – when the torment was too much to bear – would he go off the rails.

He also started to spend more time with Heather. Mostly, he talked to her about his music, playing her the songs he was learning, discussing the techniques he was developing, planning to purchase new accessories. Heather was a grand audience, as she never tired of his saxophone. But they would also play cards or watch television together sometimes. One weekend, he even proposed a long walk in the freshly-fallen snow. They quarrelled less, although a wall of cold formality remained between them.

All the while, Brian's musical ambitions grew. By late March, only five months into his musical career, he started playing *Take Five* by the Dave Brubeck Quartet, a terribly complex piece for a beginner. Then he set his sights ever higher, breaking his teeth on Coltrane's dizzying compositions. Each time, when he performed for his wife, she applauded and showered him with praise. He was convinced he was a musical prodigy.

Eventually, he reached a momentous decision. On a mild winter evening, with cottony flurries floating on the gentle breeze, he proposed that they drive to Mount Royal to take a hike. Heather was astonished, but gratefully consented. When they began walking through the snow-painted woods overlooking downtown Montreal, Brian got to the point.

"I've been thinking that I should quit my job," he began. "That would allow me to concentrate on my music. We can live on your salary until I get my new career off the ground. I think I have a real aptitude for this, and real talent. So why should I remain in a miserable job that kills my spirit when I can try to make a living doing something that I love? Maybe this'll be even better for me than Anthropology would have been."

Heather was speechless at first, not having expected this. She stood like a protractor, making small circles in the fresh snow with her brown leather knee boot.

"What do you think?" he pressed.

"Well... I can see why you'd consider something like that, but I'm not sure you're ready yet," she recovered.

"If I don't try, I may regret it," he responded. "Let's be frank, music has been the best thing to happen to me in a long time."

"True," Heather agreed, "but I have two concerns. First, the shop owner told us that your saxophone shouldn't be played in front of other people, remember?"

"Are you serious?" he blurted out. "Do you really believe his 'magic saxophone' tale?"

"I know it's crazy, but in a way, yes. You're playing Coltrane in only a few months, with yourself as a teacher. Doesn't that seem strange to you? It should take years to develop that kind of skill."

"Well yes, that's occurred to me. But maybe I have talent, too," he said with some annoyance.

"My second concern is more serious, though," she continued. "You know that Harry Chapin song about Mr. Tanner the cleaner? He loved singing. But was crushed and never sang again when he tried to make it as a professional, but failed. Right now, you absolutely *love* playing your sax. If you made it your job, you might lose that – especially if you didn't make it as a musician. You're happy. Why mess with that?"

He had hoped for more support. "But who says I'm going to fail? Just because I've failed at everything else....?"

"That's not what I'm saying!" she interrupted. "Let's not decide right now. Let's have this discussion again down the road. I just want to be sure that you're truly ready before you take a leap like that."

Dejected, he drove her back home and went down to his music studio to practice.

As a compromise, Heather suggested that he upgrade his accessories. It was time, she said, to get the stronger reeds and the jazz mouthpiece that were more appropriate for his music. Brian did research online and decided to buy the best equipment to help improve his sound, regardless of the cost. Heather agreed and accompanied him back to Archambault, where they bought a Vandoren V16 Metal mouthpiece for over $400 and a Francois Louis Ultimate brass ligature for another $100. Together, the salesclerk assured him, they would take his music to a completely different level. The clerk, who remembered Brian from his first visit, asked if he was ready to upgrade from his battered Selmer, but Brian said, "No. My good old saxophone will do fine."

Trying out the new accessories that evening, Brian could hear the difference immediately. He felt the tone was richer, the sound fatter. They helped him with the edgier elements of Coltrane's music. Yet, as he finished practicing he scrutinized Heather with sadness rather than elation. Behind her approving smile, he saw her in a way that he hadn't really noticed before. He saw her fatigue, her weariness, her desolation. He wondered where *her* music was. That night he drank himself to sleep again.

One night in early April, as the hard-packed snow of a Montreal winter had just begun to thaw, Brian remained alone in the basement long after he finished practicing. He was wrestling with himself, on the cusp of a profound revelation. Suddenly, he wrenched himself up and sought Heather upstairs, finding her in the room off the living room that they had designated "the baby's room" early in their marriage, which now served as her home office. He approached her with overflowing eyes.

"I'm so sad!" he drew each word out in a long, plaintive wail, the cry of a soul long smothered.

"I know. So am I."

They embraced each other in desolation. In despair. Embraced each other as they hadn't in many long, barren years. Embraced each other for an eternity, tears streaming down their cheeks, two stone gargoyles in the rain.

After several minutes, he looked at her across the gulf of his bitterness that had divided them for so long. He wanted to say more, but was in the midst of a monumental internal struggle, trying to overcome his innate reticence, the hardening of his heart that shielded him from the pain of an indifferent world.

"I think I found it at last," he said with difficulty.

"Found what, dear?"

"It's there, right in front of us, but it's covered with snow and ice."

"It's okay, Brian," she said, not fully understanding, but wanting desperately to reach him.

"*We* covered it. We didn't want to, but we *did*. We did it in spite of ourselves. *I* covered it," he moaned. "But we can try, can't we? Together?"

"Of course, Brian! Let me help you," she cried, still not comprehending.

But there was still more he wanted to say, *had* to say. He gasped for breath between his sobs, trying to compose himself. Trying to cross his Rubicon.

"Why don't we fill out an application with an adoption agency tomorrow? They'll probably reject us because we're too old. But maybe we can still be useful to a child who needs us...." he got out at last.

It was his Day of Atonement. His chance to atone for all his sins, his cruelty, his self-pity, his frailty, his failure. His humanity.

Heather was overcome by emotion, by pity, by long-spurned love. She squeezed him desperately, and they both wept, for the first time touching the depths of each other's pain. After silently rocking back and forth in each other's arms for much of the night, they eventually went to sleep, no longer as two separate broken souls, but together, as one breached, rudderless ship, hoping to reach port before the weight of the water pulls it beneath the surface forever.

After that night, he stopped drinking.

A few days later, Brian's brother from Halifax visited Montreal on a business trip and stopped at their home unannounced. He had taken to dropping in without notice, since of late Brian would always find an excuse not to see him if he called in advance. Heather answered the doorbell and invited him in while Brian was still playing saxophone in the basement. It was the first time anyone other than Heather had heard Brian play. His brother was stunned by the horrible din.

"My word, Heather!" he exclaimed, as he sat at the kitchen table, a steaming coffee mug in hand. "Is that what he's been doing all this time? He can't play a single note! He's got no rhythm! It doesn't sound like he's even blowing into the mouthpiece properly! He's just *awful!!!* How can you *stand* that awful *noise*?"

"Please don't say anything, Hank! Just leave it alone," Heather pleaded, with something approaching panic in her voice.

Hank was flummoxed. "What do you mean? All I hear when I speak to him is how great a musician he is. How he could quit his job to perform. But he has absolutely *zero* music sense. He can't play *at all*! What is *wrong* with you two?"

She regained her composure and replied gently with a sad, sly smile, "Please don't tell him! *He* doesn't know, and that's just fine with me. For whatever reason, he can't hear how badly he plays. He thinks he's Coltrane. And you know what, Hank? I think that horrible noise is the sweetest music I've ever heard."

Bonnie and Clyde

"We'll be arriving in Kingston shortly. Kingston next." the driver's tinny voice reverberated over the loudspeaker.

I must have been dozing, as his announcement startled me, making me drop the book that was precariously balanced on my lap. As I bent to retrieve it, I glanced out the grimy window and noticed that the bucolic farms of the countryside had given way to the outskirts of the city, dotted with businesses and small homes.

My coach was the early Voyageur express, departing Toronto at 8:00AM, stopping in Kingston's intercity bus depot for thirty minutes at 11:00AM. With sparse traffic that bright, lazy July morning and no construction delays, however, the bus had arrived early, and the driver informed us that we'd have almost an hour in Kingston. With nothing better to do, I decided to visit the restaurant and read until the waitress brought me the green salad and Perrier I ordered.

As I began to nibble at my salad, a girl at the entrance caught my eye. She was pretty, although not excessively so. But there was something arresting in the way she held herself, her confident demeanour. Besides, a seventeen-year-old boy didn't need any special reason to notice an attractive young woman. Eavesdropping, I heard the hostess tell her that she was sorry, but there were no free tables. Noticing that I was watching, the girl responded without hesitation, "Oh, but my boyfriend's already been seated." With that, she strode up to my table, sat down opposite me and complained, "I've been looking for you *everywhere*! Why didn't you wait for me before ordering?"

Amused and more than a little excited, I played along. "You always take forever putting your make-up on. I was *hungry*, dear."

With a grimace, she picked up her fork, reached across and skewered some of my salad. "That's just like you, always thinking with your stomach! Now we'll have to split *this* until they take *my* order."

We sat facing each other and appraised one another, like objects in a curio shop. I'd like to say she was beautiful – in my mind's eye she was – but, if I'm honest, that would be a romantic embellishment. In point of fact, she would have had a rather plain face if it hadn't been for her radiant eyes and her playful, mischievous, resplendent smile. Her head was adorned by shoulder-length dirty blonde hair, parted on the left and kept in place by a slightly cracked, brown plastic headband. Her off-white t-shirt, with the prophetic orange caption "Dynamite!" revealed a slim, fairly athletic build, with shapely, tanned legs protruding from her beige shorts. But, although she was certainly pleasant to look at, it was her eyes, which shone with the brightness of a thousand suns, that captivated my attention.

After she munched through half my salad, the waitress arrived to take her order. "It's a bit early for lunch," she mused, "I'll just have a large chocolate milkshake with two straws." When the waitress retreated, I tried to introduce myself to my newfound companion. "I'm__" But she cut me off. "No names, okay? I'm Bonnie; you're Clyde." I nodded my surprised assent.

We exchanged some more faux-couple banter, then talked for a bit about nothing in particular: rock bands, television, and the like. Typical teenager fare. I told her I loved Springsteen, John Cougar, Pink Floyd, the Melancholy Grapes. "Oh! Too sad! I like songs that don't make me want to suck a tailpipe."

"Like what?" I asked, perhaps a little condescendingly.

"Anything by the Beach Boys. A lot of Beatles songs. Or how about *Walking on Sunshine*? Every time I hear it, it just makes me want to get up and dance!"

"Yeah, it's a great dance song," I agreed, "but it's not very sophisticated."

"Who needs sophisticated, Clyde, if it makes you want to cry? Life's about feeling good."

"Maybe some of the time," I demurred, "but it can also be sad and dark. And lonely. I like the poetry in Springsteen's songs, the raw emotion in the Melancholy Grapes. They give voice to the poor, the miserable, the downtrodden."

"Oh, come on!" she snapped. "What's the appeal of a song like *The River*, where the singer lives a hopeless life of drudgery because of one mistake? Or *Badlands*. He waits his whole life for something that never comes. What's uplifting about that? Or *Haunted* by the Grapes, *"Life is a disease, it'll bring you to your knees."* Life isn't all hardship and misery. It can be fun. And hopeful!"

"You certainly know your Springsteen and Melancholy Grapes for someone who *dislikes* their music," I quipped.

"Of course I know it. Springsteen's a brilliant poet of despair. And his music is nice. Same with the Grapes. But why do we need more despair?" she asked.

I took a mocking tone, "So you prefer the subtle artistry of *Walking on Sunshine*, with its ungrammatical lyrics punctuated by a healthy dollop of wo-ohs?"

"Every day of the week! Sure, there's sadness and darkness in the world, but what good does it do to wallow in it? I'd rather focus on the sunshine and feeling good. Wouldn't you?" She said this with the air of someone who had partaken of her share of sadness, but had chosen not to let it defeat her. That moved me. But as a glass-half-empty person, I didn't quite know how to respond, so I just kept silent and picked at my salad.

After a few minutes, I tried to change the subject. "What programs do you watch? I really like *Hill Street Blues*," I said.

"Yeah, that fits.... It's a good show, but again, too dark. I like shows that make me laugh, like *Family Ties* or *The Cosby Show*."

"I like them too. But sometimes I want something with a bit more... well, substance," I countered.

"If by substance you mean dark and depressing, then I don't see the point."

"Those sitcoms aren't very realistic. Whatever 'horrible' thing happens – Oh no! Rudy's goldfish died!" I mimed a goldfish suffocating to illustrate my point, which brought out a laugh from her that could chase storm clouds away, "the Huxtables can laugh their way through!"

"You're a really cute dying goldfish, Clyde, but you need to loosen up!" she said, still smiling.

She paused for a few seconds, with a gleam spreading across her radiant orbs and a wrinkle in her brow as her grin grew to envelope her face. Suddenly, she reached across and touched my hand excitedly. "You know what Clyde? You're a bit too dark. You could stand to let loose a bit. You need to remember the good things in life. You need to embrace joy and hope. Let's go downtown today and have some fun."

I was taken aback. To begin with, I didn't like her describing me as "dark." More importantly, I didn't know her at all, and was unfamiliar with Kingston, which I had always unfairly viewed as dangerous because of tales I'd heard as a kid about convicts escaping from the Kingston Penitentiary. At the same time, my blood was racing. This would be spontaneous. An adventure. With a firecracker of a girl. And her magnificent hand was touching mine....

Still, true to my nature, reason got the better of me. "I'd... I'd love to," I stammered, "but I really can't. My grandparents are expecting me in Montreal and the bus leaves in about 10 minutes."

"You *can't*, or you *won't*?" 'Bonnie' challenged me. I kept my silence, unwilling to be drawn. "Look, I don't want to push you. If you don't want to spend the day with me, don't. But I like you, Clyde, and I think we'd have a blast. Why don't you call your grandparents and tell them you missed your bus and that the next bus with an open seat won't arrive until tonight? That'd give us the whole day."

She was so enticing and spoke so earnestly that her optimism overcame my innate caution. Although it was completely out of character – I was so responsible and buttoned-down – I marched anxiously to the payphone in the waiting room and complied, to my grandmother's disappointment. I didn't tell Bonnie that I also called my mother in Toronto, whose response was less generous.

I then retrieved my backpack from the luggage hold of my bus, which had not yet departed, and stuffed it in a locker at the depot, keeping a small knapsack with me.

When I returned, her face glowed. "All free now, Clyde?" she asked triumphantly.

"I am," I replied, more than a little nervous now that the cord was cut.

"Good! Now what should we do?" She asked, as she passed me a straw to share the milkshake that had arrived in my absence.

After a minute's thought, I suggested, "I suppose we could see a movie. Or go bowling." I could see from her face that I was fishing in the wrong stream.

"BOOO-RING!!" she crowed. "Come on, Clyde! Today is a gift that neither of us expected to have. Let's have fun with it. Let's live it like it's our last day on Earth."

"Okay, but what do you want to do?" It seemed best to let her suggest something, since anything I proposed would be deemed boring. And, to be honest, I probably wasn't the best person to plan a fun day.

"Well…" she began playfully, "I want to do something really *crazy* before the day is done."

That made me somewhat uneasy. Although by this point I clearly liked her, I didn't need my curmudgeonly parents to point out the potential dangers. I knew nothing about her, not even her name. What if she *was* crazy? Or worse?

She was sublimely aware of the affect she was having on me, and from her oversized grin, seemed to enjoy keeping me off balance.

"What are you afraid of? Do you think I want to rob a bank, Clyde?" She held out her forefinger with her thumb pointing up, ordering me to "stick 'em up!" I put my hands in the air and pretended to be frightened. With a sly look, she leaned forward and quickly kissed my lips. The effect on me was electric. The scent of her hair. Her nose gently caressing my cheek as she leaned in. The touch of her soft puckered lips to mine. Her magnificent, easy charm. It was more than I could resist. To a repressed teenager who had spent the last three years in a private, boys-only high school, who had scant experience with the fairer sex, Bonnie was manna straight from heaven. Playful. Intelligent. Adorable. Uninhibited. I fell deeper and deeper in love with her with each passing minute.

"I know, let's lift something from Eaton's!" She suddenly blurted out.

My face fell. What was I getting myself into? Perhaps she was trouble after all. "Are you crazy?" I almost shouted. An elderly couple at the next table glared at us disapprovingly.

"Just kidding! Wow, I really had you going there. You're all red! Don't worry, I'm no thief. Seriously, though, it's a sunny day and I need some shades if we're gonna have fun outdoors. Let's start off by shopping downtown and then move on to other things."

It suddenly occurred to me to ask how old Bonnie was, since I was too young to drink if her plans were to include that. Age had always been a touchy subject for me. Having skipped grade 2 and completed grades 11 and 12 in the same year, I was perpetually a year or more younger than the girls in my cohort. Since community social events were typically stratified by grade, I always found myself attracted to girls with scant interest in a little brother.

She summarily shut me down. "No boring questions. Besides, why would that possibly matter? Age is just a number. If you like me as a person and we get along, does it matter if I'm fifteen or twenty? I'm still the same person."

"That's what I always say!" I gasped. "You're the first person I've met who sees it my way, though."

"People are so obsessed with age, with money, with status, that they fail to see what's *really* important. What's inside someone," Bonnie declared, as she adjusted her headband. "And it makes no difference whether anybody agrees with you. You can be right even when the whole world disagrees. Of course, you need to listen to what they're saying to see if it makes sense. But if it doesn't, just forget 'em."

She dazzled me. Who was this self-confident, clear-thinking girl? The afternoon promised to be memorable.

We rode a city bus to the downtown shopping area. Our first stop actually *was* Eaton's department store. We wandered through the music section, checking out the latest records, listening to the tunes playing on a stereo to attract customers.

"There's a new album by Dire Straits. I really liked some of their earlier songs," I commented.

"No doubt *Telegraph Road* was one of them. That sounds depressing enough for you," she teased.

"Actually yes. It's one of my favorite songs," I replied.

"Don't get me wrong. The music's great. But the lyrics are dreary and desolate."

All of the sudden, her face brightened. "Hey, they're playing *Walking on Sunshine*! Let's dance!"

In the middle of the store, she began to dance as she would have in a discotheque, with zest and abandon. I noticed a woman passing by with a bemused smile, the music department's sales-clerk monitoring us uneasily. It made me self-conscious in the extreme. But Bonnie was unfazed. She grabbed my arm and said "*You've* got to dance with me. This is our song, dear. *Forget* about everybody else; it's just you and me."

So there I was, a repressed, socially-awkward seven-teen-year-old boy dancing – more accurately hopping clumsily from foot to foot, as I was no John Travolta – in a fairly busy department store with the most beguiling girl I had ever met, belting out every single *wo-oh* at the top of my lungs. Bonnie looked radiant, her face slightly flushed, her wavy hair rippling as she bounced, her shapely legs calling out to me with every jump.

When the music ended, she tenderly chided me. "Don't worry too much about what people think. They're *probably* thinking that they wish *they* could let loose and have fun, too. If they don't... well, it's not your fault that they're dead inside. You've got to live your life to the fullest and forget about them. Now let's go get our shades."

We must have tried on every pair of sunglasses in the acces-sory department. Bonnie hammed it up, making funny faces and feigning exotic accents with the more outlandish pairs. Saying things like, "I *must* have Javier bring the Rolls into the *ga*-rage" and "Eef you don't do as you're told, we goona have to keel you!" She pushed the gaudier frames onto my face herself, with each incidental caress making my heart more and more her captive.

We each bought a cheap $3 pair of plastic sunglasses that, in Bonnie's words, "would do the trick and look killer too." Then, as we left the accessory section, her eyes fell upon an expensive pearl gray silk kerchief that would highlight her dazzling sapphire blue eyes. She looked entranced by it, and I was overcome by the impulse to give it to her.

"I'd like to buy it for you," I said, trying to constrain the emotion in my voice, but she bristled.

"Oh no! I don't want you to buy me anything! That would *ruin* it," she snapped. "I don't like gifts; I like people. Gifts are a way people who don't care about others pretend they actually do. Or a way to buy someone's affection. If I don't like you because of who you are, I'm certainly not going to like you because of some trinket you throw at me. And I don't want you to cheapen our relationship by putting a price tag on it."

"Okay!" I said guiltily, feeling rather crass. "I didn't mean to insult you."

She gently brushed my cheek with the tips of her fingers. "I know. You're sweet, Clyde. Just be yourself and you're gonna be fine."

I found myself in awe of her. She had a wisdom far beyond her youth, with clearly thought-out, unshakeable, often iconoclastic opinions about the world. Everything about her was bewitching.

As we exited the store, Bonnie seemed agitated. On the sidewalk outside, I found her fiddling with the clasp on her shoulder bag and pulling something out. To my horror, it was the gray kerchief! She *had* shoplifted after all, and I had been her unwitting accomplice. I looked around furtively, wondering what I should do.

Bonnie was exultant. "I *did* it! I've always wanted to steal something. What a rush! Now we've got to bring it back."

"What?" I exploded. "You've gotten us into big trouble. You can't go back in there!" All I could imagine now, instead of starting university in the fall, was a prison sentence.

"Well, of course I need to give it back. I'm no thief! I can't believe you'd think I am!" With that, she did an abrupt pirouette and strode back into the store, straight to the cash. I followed behind dumbly, quite agitated, expecting the worst.

"Excuse me," Bonnie addressed the cashier. "I was just in this store and, somehow or other, mistakenly left with this kerchief in my bag. I'm so embarrassed!"

The cashier collected the kerchief, checked the tag and said, "Yes, that's ours. Don't worry, honey. If you'd intended to steal it, you certainly wouldn't be bringing it back now, would you? Thanks for noticing and being so honest."

On the way out of the store, Bonnie gave me a mischievous wink.

It was *my* turn to reprimand *her*. "Honestly, Bonnie, I don't *understand* you! On one hand, you're the most intelligent person I know. You've obviously got a bright future ahead of you. Yet you do some pretty hairbrained things. Why would you risk throwing it all away on a stunt like that?"

"Oh, come on! Life's about taking risks. It's not worth living if you don't. I didn't hurt anybody, and never planned on keeping it."

Her defiant response didn't satisfy me. So she laid it all out for me. "Look, if you want to go back to your bus, you can. But if you want to try to have some fun, I'd be happier if you stayed with me. You decide."

I had half a mind to get clear and return to the bus depot. It would have been the responsible choice. By this point, however, her effect on me was too powerful. I was angry with her, but didn't want to leave her, no matter how prudent it might be.

"If you promise not to do anything else that could get us arrested, I'll *think* about it," was my eventual petulant reply.

"Yes, of course! I promise." She said brightly.

"Understand me, though. I take promises very seriously. If you give me your word, I expect you to keep it," I responded severely.

"I give you my word."

I snorted and started walking down the street, still brooding about her shoplifting. She followed a few paces behind me, a troubled look on her face. After a few minutes, she sidled up to me and took my hand in hers, stroking it with her free hand. It surprised me that she kept her nails boyishly clipped, without any polish.

She offered an apology. "You're right, Clyde, and I'm sorry. It was wrong of me to do that without consulting you first. I was selfish and inconsiderate. Please forgive me. I won't do anything like that again without asking you. Alright?"

The concern in her eyes was apparent, the quaver in her voice sincere. How could I not forgive her? I nodded my assent, and we walked quietly hand-in-hand for a few minutes, before resuming our adventure as if nothing had transpired, the privilege of the young.

The rest of that early afternoon is a blur. We walked through most of the downtown core, stopping in at several stores and buying ice cream at Baskin Robbins. We climbed the statue of John A. McDonald in City Park until a police officer ordered us to clear away. Walking on the Waterfront Trail, we skipped stones into the St. Lawrence River. We did a thousand different things, each of which would seem trivial, but for the fact that we did them together, on a day we had never expected to share.

Near the river, at McDonald Park, we sat in the grass and enjoyed a late picnic lunch, eating the sandwiches from my daypack that I had prepared for my bus ride. We lazed in the grass afterwards, talking about music and watching passersby. I decided this was a good opportunity to move beyond approved, "non-boring" topics and really get to know her. I asked her whether she would attend school in the Fall, but again she rebuffed me.

"Listen, if you want, we can have a conversation like adults do about school and work and money and responsibilities All that boring stuff. I'd rather enjoy our adventure," she explained.

"Time is running out on our adventure, and I don't even know your real name! It's four-thirty and my bus to Montreal leaves at eight. If we don't talk seriously now, our one-day adventure will remain just that. I don't want that to happen!"

Her expressive eyes hinted at some great turmoil beneath the surface of her composed face. She squeezed my hand and murmured, "You're sweet. Don't worry, we'll deal with that later." Suddenly, her expression brightened, and she cooed, "Hey, let's go ride our horse into the sunset!"

"What horse?" I queried, but she was already up and running toward a wrought iron statue of a lion on the grass, a short distance from us.

Bonnie mounted the lion's back and pretended to ride it like a horse, screaming "Giddyup!"and "Hiyo Silver!" She beckoned me to join her, so I jumped on behind her, wrapping my arm around her slender waist. I could feel her every intake of breath, my knees only inches from the back of her tanned legs, tantalizingly close to heaven. In ecstasy. In agony. I held her in trepidation while we rode through the Wild West on our trusty lion, too terrified to pull her close to me, to press my lips to the back of her head.

Our ride over, we dismounted our leonine steed. As we clambered down, my hand brushed against her knee, not entirely by accident. She smiled shily and grasped my hand, bringing it gently to her lips, sending a tremor down my spine.

"What should we do now?" she asked softly. "Do you want to take the ferry to Wolfe Island?"

"Do we have time?" The prospect of being out on the water with the wind blowing through her hair appealed me to immensely, but I was growing ever aware that our time was winding down.

"No, I suppose not," she admitted. "But we should finish off our day with something wild."

At this point, I wasn't interested in anything wild. The only fitting end to our day would have been making sure that other glorious days would follow. So I responded, tongue firmly in cheek, "Well, we could go to a nearby apartment building and throw rocks off the roof. That wouldn't be boring, would it?"

"I like it! That's something I've never done before!" she crowed with exaggerated brightness. "You're finally starting to loosen up." I decided not to tell her that I was being sarcastic.

We made our way slowly to Brock St., where Bonnie found the building she decided was ours. We approached the entrance, but it was locked. So we waited outside until we observed a tenant about to exit. Then we walked to the door, pretending we were visiting a relative.

"What's Auntie Ethyl's apartment number?" Bonnie asked me loudly.

"I don't remember. It's on the sixth floor. I'll recognize it when I see it," was my equally loud reply.

The departing woman in her prim brown frock held the door open for us with a curt nod and we were in. We were about to board the elevator, when the noise of a door slamming on the ground floor spooked Bonnie. She pulled me away toward the staircase and we raced up the first seven floors, laughing loudly, feeling the intoxicating high of doing something forbidden. We ascended the remaining floors more slowly and came to the roof access after the fifteenth floor. I was about to throw it open, when Bonnie stopped me suddenly, warning, "It might be alarmed!"

Shrugging, I thrust it open anyway, taking my chances, my heart pounding. No alarm sounded. Triumphantly, we stormed the rooftop, breathing heavy sighs of relief. The panorama of the city and the river beyond in the late afternoon sun was breathtaking to our young eyes, and we drank it in. Then Bonnie picked up some pebbles from the gutter at the edge of the roof.

"We have to be careful not to hurt anybody or damage any cars," she said. "I promised not to do anything too dangerous."

Exploring the rooftop, we discovered that one side of the building was bordered by a vacant lot, overgrown with grass. That was our safest target.

Bonnie held onto my arm to steady herself and hurled a pebble, shouting "Kawabunga!!!!"

I took a pebble from her hand and screamed, "Hey, Kingston, this is from Bonnie and Clyde!!!" as I launched it in the air. It was exhilarating.

We threw a few more pebbles, screaming with delight each time until Bonnie declared, "That's enough. I don't want to get you arrested after promising to be good."

We silently admired the view for a few more minutes before Bonnie asked, "Wasn't that a rush?"

I studied her face before replying, "Yes, it was. But *you're* a bigger rush." It was the closest I could get myself to what I really wanted to say. She enveloped me in her arms, and we held each other quietly, tenderly, each of us thinking of our approaching deadline.

Too soon, Bonnie inspected her watch like a prisoner awaiting the gallows and announced, "We'd better get back to our bus soon." *Our* bus, I observed gratefully. Not *your* bus. So at least she might be staying with me until Montreal. We descended from the roof, left our apartment building, and returned by bus to the depot.

We sat in the bus depot's restaurant, at the same table we had occupied that morning, waiting for the late bus to Montreal. No longer strangers, we sat close together and talked less, preferring to gaze into each other's eyes, each harbouring our private thoughts about the future. Since she'd be joining me on my bus, I concluded that there was still time to talk seriously later, after our Kingston adventure was over. Bonnie, however, seemed especially agitated, breathing heavily, storm clouds gathering in her eyes.

Suddenly, she glanced at her watch again and commanded, "Stand up, close your eyes and count to thirty, Clyde."

"Why?" I asked.

"Just do it for me, please."

I complied and, when I reached five, I could feel the warmth of her body getting closer, her gentle breath caressing my face. Her nervous lips parted mine and I tasted her tongue as it explored my mouth. It was my first real kiss. I opened my eyes and was surprised to witness a tear rolling down her cheek. But she complained, "You're cheating! Please keep 'em closed for me until you hit thirty." So I shut my eyes again and continued counting slowly in my head, savouring her scent, the touch of her lips, the desperate passion of her kiss, until I reached fifteen, when I felt her pull away from my mouth. When I opened my eyes at thirty, she was gone.

I was bewildered, but sat down, revelling in the tender afterglow of our kiss, expecting some new surprise from her. With each passing minute, however, my anxiety grew. After about twenty minutes, I paid our bill and left the restaurant to search for her elsewhere in the station. In the half hour before my bus departed, I looked around the bus depot and parking lot frantically – I even asked a woman to search the ladies' room for me – but failed to locate her. Eventually, feeling a pain unlike any I had known in my young life, I collected my overnight bag from the locker room and boarded my bus to Montreal, hoping against hope that she was waiting for me inside. To my everlasting sorrow, she was not.

In the years that followed, I returned to that bus depot restaurant on every trip to Montreal until I moved to Vancouver in 1990 for graduate school. After I started my first job in Montreal in 2000, I continued to break up driving trips to Toronto with a lunch stop at the restaurant in the new inter-city bus terminal that replaced my precious depot – often with my wife and sons, without explaining why – as a sort of pilgrimage, in search of I know not what. Bonnie? Some sort of closure? My lost youth? I truly can't say. For even we cannot fathom all the mysteries of our own imperfect souls.

To this day, I don't know anything about her: her name, where she lived, what she was doing at the bus station. Why did she abandon me without saying goodbye, without giving me her phone number, without letting me find her again? Had I been her only Clyde, or were there others before and after me? Did she think of me at times, or had I been erased by years of joys, heart-aches and the drumbeat routine of everyday life? Is the memory of our too brief day together as precious a gem to her as it is to me? All I know is that I had touched the stars, only to crash to the ground, never to look upon them again.

The Morning Commute

Traffic was lighter than usual that Wednesday morning along Montgomery Avenue. That could be a problem, Marcus fretted. The police had stepped up their presence on this central thoroughfare of suburban Philadelphia in recent weeks, and this stretch had become something of a speed trap. *Wouldn't do to have a brush with the law*, he reflected with a shudder. With a heavy volume of traffic he wouldn't need to worry, but this morning he'd need to be careful not to exceed the prescribed twenty-five-mile-per-hour speed limit by too large a margin.

If only he didn't have his new glasses to contend with. The optometrist had told him that she could have given him a prescription for bifocals that would have assisted with reading as well as distances. But for Marcus that was a bridge he wasn't yet ready to cross, so he consented only to driving glasses that would reduce the blurriness of the world outside his windshield.

He wasn't that old yet, was he? Fifty-five years. Most of his life had passed him by already, like so much scenery on the side of a highway, to be viewed from a safe distance but never experienced. Never married. No children. Not even many love interests to speak of over all that barren, desolate time. Instead, he put all his energy, his misguided soul, into his career. But in ten or fifteen years that will have passed, too. He will transition from *being* an engineer to *having been* one, and his insignificant life will lurch towards its unceremonious conclusion. *And what will remain from all my hard work then*, he sighed, squeezing the steering wheel with his small, dark, already wrinkled hands.

"Christ!" he cursed aloud. His new spectacles disoriented him each time he shifted his focus from the windshield to the speedometer and back. It was impossible for him to monitor his speed without lifting his glasses to enable him to read the small, nearby display. Yet his eyes needed a second or two to adjust to the lenses each time he replaced them. In the process, he almost failed to notice that the car ahead of him stopped suddenly. The piercing sunlight as he headed eastbound toward the city on this peerless autumn morning only compounded his disorientation. He slammed on his brakes just in time. *That was close*, he thought, exhaling heavily. *Now if only I could make it to work on time for the morning meeting....*

A little further up the avenue, Wade picked his way with his size-eleven loafers along the far-too-narrow sidewalk to his Bala Cynwyd practice, smiling, humming to himself. Already in his early forties, he still approached life with zest. As a challenge to be met, a sumptuous banquet to be savored. Nothing could dim the lustre of his luminous emerald eyes. Not the constricted walkway, obstructed here and there by slanted, poorly-maintained wooden electrical poles and assaulted by overgrown shrubbery so that it was a challenge to navigate without stepping onto the road or exposing a limb to the cars whizzing by in their own much-too-cramped lanes. Not the blistering argument he had had that morning with Rachel over breakfast.

After ten years of marriage, his wife had begun to resent his wandering eye and passed up no opportunity to castigate this sin. This morning's complaint? That at the dinner party with the Robinsons the previous evening, he lavished far too much attention on their hosts' attractive young neighbor, Ms. Porter, who teaches history at a local high school. Why is she so touchy all of a sudden? She knew he liked women, adored them, obsessed over them. So he likes to flirt. Big deal! But he always comes home to her at the end of the day, doesn't he?

He passed a red maple tree on the opposite side of the street, its fiery rust and pomegranate foliage glistening in the sunlight. Autumn in the neighborhood never failed to take his breath away. Yet, his attention fixed on the foliage, he nearly lost his footing and fell into the traffic as he teetered on the edge to circumvent a pole that bisected the sidewalk, leaving almost no passage for pedestrians. *Whew! That was a close call! I need to be more careful on this treacherous stretch.*

In a driveway at the end of the block, Annie had just returned from walking Zephyr, her boisterous Saint Bernard. Although she ordinarily delighted in these early morning promenades, on this occasion her humour was dark. *Why does he have to be so Goddamn condescending,* she pouted. She resented her husband's patronizing lecture about tying the dog up to the gate during her morning exercises. Sure, he had a point. Their L-shaped driveway, which was sheltered on all sides by dense shrubs, opened at the tip of the base onto Montgomery Avenue, separated from the road only by the thinnest strip of sidewalk. He worried that, left loose, the dog might charge into the street and be killed. And sure, she *was* a tad absentminded and *had* left Zephyr untethered on occasion when she got distracted. But he didn't have to treat her like a child, did he?

Besides, that was just the tip of the iceberg. She was growing resentful of her much older husband. He was always irritable, completely absorbed in his work. And he never had time to cuddle or.... Indeed, most of the time he seemed completely insensitive to her considerable charms. For him, sex was like everything else in his life. Regulated like clockwork. Once a week, every Saturday night, no innovation, no spontaneity. Didn't Jewish tradition require the man to satisfy his wife, to meet *her* needs? Sometimes she wondered why she'd married him in the first place.

She attached Zephyr's leash to the gate just as Wade approached the driveway. "Hi Annie!" he called.

She smiled – her first genuine smile of the day – and waved him up the driveway with her long, elegant arms. She'd always fretted that her limbs were too thin and gangly, but men seemed to find them enchanting. "How're you doing today, Wade?" she inquired.

"Well, I *was* okay. But now that I see you, I'm *awesome*," Wade gushed.

"Aren't you the charmer?" Annie asked sarcastically, a magenta hue painting her cheeks.

"Zephyr seems to think so." Wade had presented the back of his hand to the dog for inspection. After sniffing it, Zephyr signaled his approval by slobbering all over it, yelping happily. Wade tousled the fur on the dog's neck, causing the beast to whimper with delight. "He acts like he's just a puppy."

"He *is*," Annie affirmed. "He's only a year old. They grow quickly."

"That young? But he's huge!"

"Yeah. Already a hundred and thirty pounds. He's my little monster," Annie laughed.

They had met only the previous week, as Annie was retrieving her trash can from the curb with Zephyr at her heels during Wade's morning commute. Clad in her tight-fitting coral yoga pants and matching exercise bra, her long blonde hair hanging low, she immediately caught his eye, receptive as it always was to an attractive woman. A glib comment always at the ready, he remarked, "That's a fine-looking dog. Not as fine as his mistress, mind you." While that type of come-on would have left her cold at other stages of her life, in her present circumstances, feeling dismissed, neglected, invisible even, it was simply gratifying to be noticed. Since then, she made herself available every day after Jerry left for the office and Wade hadn't failed to stop to banter, to laugh for a few minutes each morning. There's nothing wrong with it, she assured herself. It's just harmless flirting.

The following morning, Marcus decided to try another route to work and found himself stuck on the Schuylkill Expressway. It had seemed like a good idea. Since Montgomery Avenue was treacherous, why not use the highway? But traffic on the

Schuylkill, which had been constructed long before the explosion of cars in the city, was sluggish at the best of times. All the more so during the morning commute. *Oh well,* he sighed resignedly. *There's not much I can do about it now. At least there's no risk of getting a ticket here.*

Suddenly, amidst the crowd of commuters in their separate metal boxes, he felt more isolated, more forsaken than ever before. *I'm so lonely,* he sighed pitifully. *It's strange how you can feel more alone surrounded by all of humanity than you do with no-one around.... Perhaps I should ask Scott if he wants to watch the Eagles game with me at the bar on Sunday. It's better than watching alone, I suppose.* Then, composing himself, he walked himself through his plan for the nine o'clock meeting with his boss. He was never fully at ease in that all-white company. Always felt like he had to justify their faith in him by going beyond what was expected. When he arrived twenty minutes late for the meeting, however, he cursed softly and swore that he'd revert to his usual route in the future.

On Montgomery Avenue, Wade was enjoying his morning visit with Annie. Although he wore his professional twill pants, he practically kneeled on the asphalt to give a belly rub to Zephyr, who upon seeing his new friend stretched out on his back, his paws in the air.

"He's such a slut," Annie guffawed.

"You can't blame him," Wade countered with a naughty wink. "I *do* have magic hands."

"Magic hands...." Annie repeated thoughtfully. "I wish there *were* such things."

"Why," he asked. "What's wrong?"

"Oh, nothing," she responded quickly. "I just strained my neck with these stretches."

Wade burst into a wide grin. "Well, this is fate or karma or something. I just happen to be Bala Cynwyd's best chiropractor! Sit down and let me take a look."

Annie was taken aback. "Well, I don't know...."

"C'mon. It's what I do for a living," he insisted.

Annie glanced around uneasily, grateful that the neighbors' prying eyes were held in check by thick walls of shrubs on all sides. "I suppose it couldn't hurt," she said shyly. Then she squatted down on the pavement and crossed her long legs.

Wade ran his fingers along the back of her neck and shoulders. "Wow, you're very tense. You need to loosen up more," he opined, as he began to pull gently on her neck. Then he eased her onto her back and began moving her neck from side to side.

"I'm not gonna let you give *me* a belly rub, though," Annie said nervously. "You'll have to stick to Zephyr for that."

"Deal!" he responded. After manipulating her neck in figure-eight rotations, Wade lifted her back into a sitting position, inserted his hands underneath her loose-fitting t-shirt and massaged her shoulders, the top of her back, noting with excitement that he encountered no bra strap, as Zephyr whined impatiently.

Annie emitted a deep and pleasurable sigh, simultaneously relaxed and aroused. "Wow!" she exclaimed demurely. "You really *do* have magic hands."

He withdrew from her back slowly, caressing her silky skin as he did so, furtively glancing through the widening gap in the front of her shirt, now that he was no longer pulling the material backward, at her unencumbered breasts. Raising her to her feet, he bowed gallantly and took his leave for the day, chanting, "Well, I owe. I owe. So it's off to work I go."

"Oh. I'll see you tomorrow then, doctor," Annie said with a sly giggle, her face glowing. "The patient may need your services again."

As he marched down the driveway to the sidewalk, Zephyr yapping in his wake, Wade was buffeted by an admixture of titillation and shame. *Maybe I took this too far,* he considered. *It's okay to flirt, but this is farther than I've gone before. It's not really fair to Rachel. I still love her, despite it all.*

After raining heavily all night, the air was still damp, the driveway slick on Friday morning when Annie kissed her husband goodbye for the day, a perfunctory, business-like peck on the cheek. She quickly rushed back inside, her heart racing, to change clothing. Off went her frumpy jeans and baggy top, on went her revealing red halter top and her skimpy ivory tennis skirt. She hesitated for an instant. It was too cold to exercise in that. But after his massage yesterday, wearing it for him was all she could focus on all day and, more importantly, throughout the interminable, sleepless night, with her husband snoring sterilely beside her. She even toyed with the idea of feigning a calf strain, or perhaps something higher up, and letting him apply his magic fingers to that part of her anatomy.

She filled Zephyr's bowl self-consciously and began to limber up with a few stretches, flushing crimson as she realized just how much she was revealing. *You can't seriously be doing this, Annie*, she chided herself. *You're acting like a schoolgirl. For God's sake! You're thirty-three years old!* Yet she stubbornly resisted the impulse to cover up. After stretching, she continued to loosen up with a few laps around the stem of the L-shaped driveway, Zephyr padding closely behind.

Just then, she heard her telephone ringing. *Damn! Left it inside.* Rushing indoors to retrieve it, she left the dog on the driveway untethered.

At that moment, Wade was cautiously navigating the narrow, obstructed sidewalk, slick with puddles and wet leaves, and approaching her house. *Wow!* he sighed. *It's tough enough when it's dry, but this is ridiculous! Especially with my large feet. One false step and I'm toast!* While he gingerly hugged an electrical pole, droplets of last night's rain still dripping from overhanging trees onto his curly chestnut hair, a smile crossed his lips as he anticipated his morning visit with Annie. But then his face immediately clouded over. *It's Rachel's birthday today. How can I keep doing this to her? Isn't it time I grew up?* He paused at the threshold of the L-shaped driveway, at war with his impulses. Then, with a heavy heart, he decided to do the right things for once and bypass her driveway. *Yes, that's the only decent thing to do.*

Meanwhile, Marcus was struggling against the glaring sun, which had peeked out from behind the clouds to wreak havoc on the roads, the narrow lanes, other commuters pushing him to accelerate to beat the light. He blasted his horn in frustration at an aggressive driver who cut him off without signaling. Still muttering, he merged into the right lane to escape from other impatient motorists. *Honestly! Is it worth risking life and limb just to arrive a few seconds earlier?* That was when, with a shiver down his spine, Marcus noticed the police car on a side street to the north, just past the light, monitoring traffic. With a start, he eased his foot off the gas pedal and consulted the speedometer, lifting his spectacles off his eyes to read the dial. *God, I hate this commute....*

Zephyr was staring at the screen door, impatiently awaiting his mistress' return. Suddenly, his tail perked up as he caught wind of a familiar scent. Away he went, bounding down the driveway toward the street to greet his friend. Wade emerged from behind the shrubs to the driveway entrance, determined to rush by it without stopping, just as the enormous dog had reached the sidewalk. He was stunned to see the beast lunge at him, tail wagging, barking happily, eager to smother him with slobber and affection. The dog's weight and momentum knocked Wade off his balance on the slippery, narrow, leaf-strewn side-walk, and they both tumbled onto the road, struggling to evade the oncoming traffic.

About four car-lengths away, Marcus's eyes were glued to the speedometer. *Only eight miles above the limit,* he noted with satisfaction. He replaced his glasses and returned his attention to the road in front of him, as his eyes slowly readjusted, too late to avoid the fumbling shapes in his path. "Christ!" he yelled, as he slammed on the brakes and instinctively swerved hard left in an attempt to avoid impact. In the process, he clipped Wade's head with the passenger-side headlight, killing him instantly. The dog caromed off the windshield and fell whimpering beside his deceased friend. Meanwhile, Marcus's head bounced between his steering wheel and the headrest, as he collided with a minivan to his left. The van, in turn, skidded into oncoming traffic across the median, causing an eight-car pile-up.

Annie hung up the phone when she saw the police car's flashing lights. "Can I call you back, Dad? It looks like something's goin' on outside." She blushed as she straightened her miniskirt and hoped she hadn't already missed Wade. Upon pushing open her screen door, she was surprised not to hear Zephyr complaining about a dearth of attention. It was then, with a sudden sinking feeling in her chest, that she noticed that he wasn't tied to the gate. Her heart in her mouth, she sprinted down the base of the L to the street. There she saw Zephyr moaning weakly amidst a twisted mass of steel and glass, his mangled frame heaving slowly next to the chiropractor's lifeless body, as a police officer struggled to extract Marcus, his head bloodied and bruised, from the glassless window of his vehicle. Straining to comprehend the magnitude of the carnage, she sunk to the pavement, sobbing uncontrollably, as the sirens of an approaching ambulance shattered the quiet of the brightening autumn morning.

Little Piece of Heaven

Misfortune had framed John's life, shaped its contours, but he never allowed it to define him. His wife died two days after giving birth to their first child, Trevor, suffering a postpartum hemorrhage while asleep in their bed at night. Her passing left a crater in John'is heart that would never be filled. Yet he needed to carry on for the baby's sake, so he re-ordered his life and his priorities, devoting himself to his son at the expense of all else, especially his career.

John had graduated near the top of his class at York's Schulich Business school and secured employment as a management consultant at one of the most prestigious Toronto firms. With his wife's death, though, he was compelled to put his career on hold, as he filed for a parental leave to care for his son. Upon returning to work six months later, although his parents and in-laws pitched in to help him out, he eschewed the late hours and travel that were essential for upward mobility in order to be home for Trevor when he returned from daycare. For this reason, despite his great talent and collegial personality, he was repeatedly passed over for raises, promotions, marquee assignments. Yet he accepted his stunted career path with equanimity, knowing it was the right choice to make for his son. Eventually, realizing that he needed more flexibility from work to manage the illnesses, doctor's visits and other unexpected obligations of a single parent, John quit the firm and started a lower-paying job as a bookkeeper at a Scarborough automotive accessories company near their apartment.

As his son grew, John remained dedicated to his happiness. They would take long walks, during which he would talk about the boy's mother, school, lizards, Harry Potter, space flight – anything that caught the boy's fancy. They would watch Maple Leaf and Blue Jays games together, parodying the ads that accompanied the broadcasts. *Sure watching hockey is fun, but wouldn't it be more fun if you impaired your senses with beer? Or, try our new laundry detergent with sulfuric acid: not only will it wash away stains, it'll dissolve your clothes, as well.*

Most of all, Trevor adored the fanciful stories that his father invented for his enjoyment. John told tales of rabbits that built an intricate underground city more beautiful that anything that ever saw the light of day; of a planet where no-one ever experienced sadness; of a kingdom where tears were more valuable than gold. Trevor always listened with rapt attention, eagerly transported to whatever world his father created for him.

Yet tragedy continued to stalk their family. One autumn, when Trevor was only eight years old, they received word that John's father had been a victim of a hit-and-run at a Scarborough crosswalk. The driver had been under the influence and did not even slow down. John's father never recovered consciousness and died in the hospital two days later.

Painful as his death was for John, he realized that it was devastating for Trevor, who adored his grandfather. After the funeral, he found Trevor in his room, crying.

"I know you're sad, Sport," he sat down on his son's bed. "I'm sad too."

"I… It's just…." the boy struggled in vain to find words to express his profound grief, his monumental sense of loss. Eventually, he settled upon "It's not *fair*, Dad!"

John gazed upon his son, marvelling at how similar they looked. The same curly, out-of-control hair, the pouty cheeks, the pointed chin, the short neck that made it look as if his head was attached directly to his chest. "I know, son," he said. "Life's not always fair. But it can also be extraordinary and wonderful. You have to accept the heartbreak – painful as it is – to be able to enjoy its beauty."

"There's *nothing* beautiful anymore, Dad," the boy howled.

"I used to think that too, Sport. But then, something happened," his father responded cryptically.

The boy perked his head up slightly, intrigued by the mystery in his father's voice. "What happened?"

"Well, I don't know if I can tell you, Sport. It's a secret," John reasoned slowly.

"Come on, Dad. You've *got* to tell me." His mood had shifted, as only a child's could. Putting aside his misery, Trevor was on tenterhooks, eager to share in his father's secret.

"I suppose I could, but only if you promised never to tell a *soul*__"

"I promise!" Trevor cut him off excitedly.

"…and you must never ask me about it either," his father continued.

"I promise! Now tell me, Dad, *please!*"

"Well, when I was young, I used to think that there was nothing but meanness and sadness in this world. But then I found something that was truly magnificent, positively *miraculous!*"

"What was it?" Trevor asked with rapt attention.

"You really can't breathe a word about this to anyone, because I'm not actually sure I'm allowed to have this," his father cautioned.

"I *won't*, Dad. But what was it?" Trevor grabbed his father's hand with both of his.

"It was…" John appeared to be struggling with himself, unsure about whether to continue. Finally, he whispered, "It was a little piece of Heaven."

"Really?" Trevor asked quizzically, apparently unsure quite what to make of this revelation.

"Yeah. Somehow it got lost and found its way down to Earth. I was lucky enough to be the one to find it. It's unbelievably exquisite and wonderful. More beautiful than anything I could ever have imagined. I took it home with me and kept it secret. Now whenever I'm sad and think that there's no point in life, I look at it and feel better. Hopeful. It gives me the strength to endure anything," John declared solemnly.

The boy's face brightened. "Can I *see* it?" he asked, his imagination captured.

"When you get older," his father assured him. "But don't ask me. *I'll* know when you're ready. Is that a deal?"

"Deal," he answered, before throwing his arms around his father and hugging him fiercely, desperately, as if he was all Trevor had left in the world.

In the years after his father's death, John lavished even more love and attention upon his son, eager to fill in for both absent mother and beloved grandfather. For his part, Trevor clung to John desperately, lest something untoward should become of him, too. Although he loved his son dearly, sometimes the burden on John was heavy. Most of the time he bore it gracefully, serenely even. Yet there were times when every sinew of his soul was stretched to the breaking point. Despite himself, he would grow short-tempered with the boy, often snapping at him for his youthful exuberance, for his smothering attention. The pained look of betrayal in Trevor's eyes on these occasions was soul-wrenching for John, and he worked hard to reign in his impatience.

In one such moment of weakness, when Trevor was nine years old, John sought release by complaining to his mother, who often helped him take care of the boy.

"I am so *drained*," he began, slumped on a kitchen chair, after putting Trevor to bed and preparing the boy's lunch for the following day.

"It's been tough on you," his mother acknowledged, her gnarled, arthritic hands playing absently with the napkin holder.

"'Tough' doesn't *begin* to describe it!" bemoaned John. "He's a handful. I mean, he's a good boy. But he's an inexhaustible ball of energy. Always climbing on the furniture, scratching the walls, breaking things. And all those *questions*! It's always 'Why? Why? Why?'"

"You were like that, too, John."

"Yeah, I suppose I was. But you had Dad to share the load with you," he mused, burying his chin into his burly chest.

"That's true. Although in those days men didn't help as much as they do now," she reflected.

"I work like a dog all day, then come home to get supper ready and help him with his homework. *You* never had to do that with *us*. Since when do parents have to spend two hours a night doing homework? I've already passed grade 4!" His mother laughed softly. "Then it's play time, story time, bedtime, and time to make lunches, do laundry, and clean up the unholy mess he's made. On the weekends, it's hockey practice or Little League. There's no time for myself! Honestly, that boy is killing me!" John wailed.

His mother cleared her throat awkwardly. Her lined face coloured a little, revealing her discomfort at intruding into her son's private life. "You know what I think, John? I think you need to start seeing people." She hesitated for a moment, clearly uncertain of how direct she should be. "Seeing women again."

"Aw, Mom. I just don't have the time."

His mother averted her eyes, fixing them on the cuckoo clock on the wall. "Is it that? Or are you afraid it'd be disloyal to Barb? She's been gone almost ten years!"

John flushed, as if he were about to explode, but then inhaled deeply and softened his expression. "I know you're concerned about me, Mom. But between work and Trevor, I can barely manage my own affairs. I just don't have the bandwidth for dating."

A sudden noise from the hallway caught their attention. With a sinking feeling in the pit of his stomach, John heard muffled sobs and the rapid padding of small footsteps, followed by the click of the bedroom door.

How long had he been eavesdropping? How much had he heard, John wondered, feeling monstrously guilty, ashamed. He vowed never to complain about Trevor again.

One Sunday, when a torrential deluge forced them to cancel a long-planned father-son horseback riding excursion, Trevor spent the morning moping in bed. When John entered the boy's room to cheer him up, he found his son more angry than sorrowful.

"I *hate* the rain!" Trevor declared with venom. It was an indictment of all that had gone wrong in his young life.

John sat down on the corner of the bed and told his son a story. "Once upon a time, there was a little boy who never met his Mommy. But *she* knew *him* very well. She watched him every day and was proud of everything he did and accomplished. But she was sad because she couldn't touch him, couldn't hug her little boy, couldn't tell him how much she loved him. So she asked an angel to teach her how to send rain down from the sky to touch her son. To give him the hugs and kisses that she always wanted to shower him with."

The boy's clever blue eyes flashed up at his father hopefully. "Do you think that Mommy's trying to hug *me?*"

"I don't know, Sport. But there's somewhere we could go to find out," his father answered.

"Where, Dad?"

"Somewhere Mommy and I liked to spend time together before you were born," was John's reply. "We loved the trees in the York University arboretum. That was our special place to escape the world. Let's go there. If she's sending the rain to reach us, I know she'd definitely send it there."

Trevor's face beamed. "Yes! Let's go now," he said with urgency, clearly forgetting his earlier frustration.

After that, the two of them could often be found in the arboretum on rainy days, staring up at the clouds far above the trees and waving, blowing kisses as the rain washed over them.

Like a dog with a juicy bone, misfortune continued to toy with John, unwilling to release his Job from his cursed grasp. On one grey late-autumn afternoon, when Trevor was fifteen years old, he returned home from high school to find their apartment building a smoking, smouldering ruin. The fire department concluded that a grease fire in another unit had spread, engulfing the entire building. In the face of yet another tragedy, John and Trevor moved in with John's mother while they sought more permanent quarters. John promised his son that they would emerge from this intact, even stronger, as they always did. But Trevor was distraught and, above all, worried, almost panic-stricken.

When they were permitted to enter the building a few days later to sift through their charred belongings, Trevor seemed disinterested in his own effects – his hockey card collection, his guitar, his sporting equipment, as if he could live without them. When his father emerged from what was left of his bedroom, Trevor probed his face for a sign that could put his mind at ease. Seeing nothing but discouragement, he could contain himself no longer.

"Did it survive? Is it safe?" he asked breathlessly.

"Huh?" his father grunted. "What do you mean?"

"The little piece of Heaven," Trevor whispered.

John smiled. "Oh, I didn't think you remembered. Yes, thank God it didn't burn. It's the first thing I checked."

The expression of relief – almost joy – on Trevor's face was heartwarming. The precious relic had survived. Against all the odds. Trevor realized now that he could endure almost all losses, provided that most sacred of legacies remained.

For several years after the fire, it appeared that misfortune had lost interest in John, that he had completed his penance and could now partake of life fully without fear of further tragedy. Trevor grew into a handsome and intelligent young man, successful in all he set his mind to. He graduated high school as the valedictorian at Sir John A. MacDonald Collegiate, winning a full scholarship to the University of Toronto, where he enrolled in University College on the St. George campus to pursue a double major in history and English literature. He excelled in sports, as well, playing on the top defence pairing of the Varsity Blues hockey team as of his second year.

As Trevor spread his wings, he began to spend more time out of the house: in school, at hockey practice, or just out with friends. He was also increasingly active socially, being extremely popular with the opposite sex. Immensely proud of his son, John never begrudged Trevor his independence and encouraged him to sample all that he could of life's sumptuous buffet. He arranged his schedule, where possible, to fit himself into the bustle of his son's life, eager to pounce on an opening whenever Trevor was available. Whenever he could, he occupied a bleacher seat at Blues' home games to cheer his son on. If Trevor was too busy with his teammates after the game to celebrate a victory or dissect a loss with his father over dinner, John would return home without complaint to prepare a meal for one instead.

Involuntarily freed from his son's orbit, John began to develop a social life of his own. He volunteered two evenings a week at the local foodbank. He visited his aging mother regularly in her assisted living facility. When the weather cooperated, he enjoyed hikes on the Scarborough Bluffs. He even started dating. It wasn't easy after so much time, nor was it exclusive, but he would occasionally enjoy dinner and a movie with a neighbour from the building, a colleague at work or a fellow foodbank volunteer to help lessen the loneliness that was his lot now that Trevor was older. In this manner, his life developed a comfortable rhythm that was not entirely unpleasant.

As it happened, however, misfortune had one more cruel trick to play on John. After suffering from a worsening cough and unexplained weight loss, John was diagnosed with mesothelioma, as a result of asbestos exposure at his first job. Around the time that Trevor was born, the company that employed John had conducted asbestos abatement in their building over a six-month period. Management assured the employees that, since the contractor was following the latest approved procedures to contain the abatement area, it was safe to work on site while the remediation proceeded. Apparently, they had been overly optimistic.

After the diagnosis, John's health deteriorated rapidly. He developed a hoarse cough and was perpetually wheezing and short of breath. Over a period of months, he lost over twelve kilograms, giving his once-burly frame a scrawny and frail aspect. Although the doctors at Princess Margaret Hospital did their utmost, with an aggressive chemotherapy regimen, it was clear that the long-term prognosis was poor, with a median survival rate of no more than ten to twelve months.

Trevor was heartbroken. He requested a leave of absence from his studies to accompany his father to each treatment session and every doctor's appointment. When possible, he stayed home to cook for his father and take his mind off his pain by watching their beloved Maple Leafs and Blue Jays, still parodying the ads as they used to. Yet the disease progressed rapidly, leaving them little time and less hope.

On a chilly Tuesday afternoon in late September, with the leaves struggling to remain on increasingly bare branches in the face of the wind's relentless onslaught, it was clear that John too was losing his tenuous grip on life. Trevor sat at his father's side in the intensive care unit of the Toronto General Hospital, trying valiantly to keep up a cheerful monologue about the weather, the Blue Jays' playoff hopes, provincial politics – anything to distract them both from the dismal, hopeless reality. John spoke infrequently by this point, as it took too much out of him.

Suddenly, tired of all the empty talk and fearing that he might not get another opportunity, Trevor blurted out, with a tremor in his voice, "I'm sorry for everything, Dad!"

"What...?" his father asked weakly, not quite comprehending.

"I'm sorry for being a burden on you all these years. I know how hard it was for you." Trevor grasped his father's frail hand in both of his, while he fought to restrain his tears.

John's gaunt face contorted in anguish, as he mustered his strength to speak. "Listen, son...." John began, struggling to control his breathing. "I need... to tell you something."

"I'm listening, Dad," Trevor whispered, as he held his father's hand over the hospital bed guardrail.

"When I was a…" John was interrupted by a coughing fit, which he struggled to contain before continuing. "When I was a young man… not much older than you… I travelled the world after I graduated from York."

John stopped speaking while he tried to prop himself up on his left elbow to face his son, causing a tremor in the intravenous tube protruding from the vein in that arm. The patient in the next bed, an elderly woman, began screaming for a nurse. Trevor wanted to visit the nursing station on her behalf, but was reluctant to leave his father, so he remained.

"I was lost.…" Every wheezing breath he took was laboured, every word slow, but deliberate. "I didn't know what I would do… with my life and was… discouraged about leaving York.…"

Trevor stroked his hand, waiting for him to continue.

"And then.… everything changed. During my travels, far away from home… I met an *angel*.…"

Trevor thought his father was delirious. "Dad. I know," he said. "I think you told me this before. About the piece of Heaven. It's just a story, though, isn't it? Just something you made up to comfort me when I was a kid. Don't waste your strength on it now."

But John seemed more determined than ever to finish. "She was perfect in every respect.… Beautiful… brilliant… kind.…" He suffered an extended coughing fit and motioned to Trevor to give him a sip of water. As Trevor did so, he was relieved to see a nurse arriving to attend to the neighbouring patient.

"Having discovered her…" John continued, "I was able to make myself a better person.…" The hollow coughing began again.

"Dad, it's okay. Why don't you rest?" Trevor beseeched him, but John silenced him with a weak motion of his trembling hand.

"I persuaded her to... marry me..." he continued with great effort, "and knew the greatest joy that... has ever been possible on earth."

John stopped for a deep, raspy intake of breath. Tears welled up in his jaundiced, glassy, hollow eyes. Trevor bit the inside of his cheek, hoping to restrain himself from crying.   "But she couldn't stay down here forever...." John resumed. "She belonged up in Heaven... with the other angels... and had to return."

"Before she went back home... she left me a small, but precious gift... the likes of which doesn't exist anywhere else on earth... She gave me my little piece of Heaven."

Trevor thrust his hands in his pockets, digging his fingernails into his palms in a fruitless effort to prevent himself from crying. All he could say in a mournful voice was "Dad...."

"It's *you*, Trevor...." John cried out at last, elated to have been able to finish, despite the pain, the difficulty breathing, the enormous expense of energy. "You're not a burden.... You've always been the little piece of Heaven... that made it possible for me to carry on."

Overwhelmed by emotion, Trevor gazed through a prism of bitter tears at his father, his hero, his everything. "No," he objected, "you've got it all wrong, Dad. Mom left *me* in the care of the kindest, sweetest angel that ever breathed on Heaven or on Earth."

But John didn't hear him, as he had fallen asleep, exhausted from the effort required to tell his final story. He never regained consciousness. A few hours later, with Trevor by his side, he suffered acute respiratory failure and hastened to leave the room to rejoin his wife.

Appendix: Song Epigraphs

1. A Weekend at the Cottage – Pearl Jam, "Black."

2. The Satchel – The Who, "Early Morning, Cold Taxi."

3. Special Delivery – Stevie Wonder, "Isn't She Lovely?"

4. Modern Love – Joni Mitchell, "Big Yellow Taxi."

5. Memory – Simon and Garfunkel, "Bookends."

6. Chat Room – Peter Gabriel, "Here Comes the Flood."

7. The Middle – Stealer's Wheel, "Stuck in the Middle With You."

8. The Siren's Call – The Moody Blues, "In Your Wildest Dreams."

9. Speculation – Crash Test Dummies, "Superman's Song."

10. The Rebellion – Leonard Cohen, "I'm Your Man."

11. The Magic Saxophone – Harry Chapin, "Mr. Tanner."

12. Bonnie and Clyde – Dire Straits, "Telegraph Road."

13. The Morning Commute – The Guess Who, "Bus Rider."

14. Little Piece of Heaven – John Lennon, "Beautiful Boy."

www.ingramcontent.com/pod-product-compliance
Lightning Source LLC
Chambersburg PA
CBHW020409210626
46816CB00006BB/2191